BOO

LEGENDS

by
Raelyn Shaye

Gotham Books

30 N Gould St.
Ste. 20820, Sheridan, WY 82801
https://gothambooksinc.com/

Phone: 1 (307) 464-7800

© 2024 *Raelyn Shaye*. All rights reserved.

No part of this book may be reproduced, stored in a retrieval system, or transmitted by any means without the written permission of the author.

Published by Gotham Books (February 28, 2024)

ISBN: 979-8-88775-832-9 (P)
ISBN: 979-8-88775-833-6 (E)

Because of the dynamic nature of the Internet, any web addresses or links contained in this book may have changed since publication and may no longer be valid.

The views expressed in this work are solely those of the author and do not necessarily reflect the views of the publisher, and the publisher hereby disclaims any responsibility for them.

CONTENTS

Corn Mystery 1
Spooky Woods 6
Haunted House 11
The Attic 16
Graveyard Hunt 21
Abandoned Mansion 26
Bat Cave 32
Creepy Road 37
Lake Dock 43
Basement Shadows 48
Tree House 53
A Town's Curse 58
Screaming Bridge 63
Killer Among Us 68
Island Scares 74
Scarecrow's Field 79
Bad Dreams 84
Rustic Caboose 89
Red Barn 94
Green Witches 99
Cruise Ship 104
Underground Tracks 109
Sewer Adventures 114
Behind the Waterfall 119
Camping Story 124
From beyond 129

CORN MYSTERY

"Once upon a time, there was a town full of little children. They played day and night. As they grew older, the disappearances began. One day, a few of the children decided to venture off. They came to a field of corn. It looked dark and scary as they approached. Growls from the field scared them and they ran off screaming. The other children couldn't believe what they were hearing, but were warned to never go near the cornfield." Timothy told his younger sister and her friends.

"Did they listen?" Allen asked.
"Hush! I'm trying to hear!" Sally exclaimed.

"Over the next few years, children began disappearing a little at a time. No adult could understand. Only the first small group of children knew that the corn was eating the children who entered the field, to never return again." Timothy continued.

"That's not a scary story!" Ben yelled out.

"It's a true story. And if you don't believe me, then go see for yourself. It's a story that has been heard through generations. When the children grew up, they warned their children of the forbidden field. No one goes near it." Timothy said.

"I'm not afraid! I will go!" Ben shouted.
"Are you crazy! The corn might eat you too!" Sarah exclaimed.
"Come on, think about it. Corn that eats kids? That's such a fake story." Ben said.
"Well, if it's fake then we will go visit it." Allen stated.

The next day, the children gathered to hike to the forbidden field. It was a couple miles outside of town on the other side of a small mountain of grass.

"There it is!" Sarah shouted.
"I see it!" Frank hollered out.
"It does look scary. Maybe we shouldn't go farther." Sally said.
"No turning back now. Let's prove this legend wrong." Ben said.

The children kept going. Once they got to the corn, they stopped.

"What are you waiting for?" Allen asked as he pointed towards the entrance of the field.
"You go in." Sarah said.
"You first!" Frank shouted to Allen.
"Everyone listen. There are no growling sounds. The story was fake." Ben said.
"Let's go home." Sally said.

They turned around to leave when all of a sudden,

"What is this I have found?" Sally asked herself as she knelt to admire what looked like a small orange object on the ground.
"Let me see!" Ben hollered out.
"It's candy." Sarah said.
"Don't eat it." Frank said.
"Why not?" Ben asked.
"Where did it come from?" Sally asked.
"I don't know." Allen said.
"Look!" Sally shouted pointing towards the field.

They all stood up and turned around.

"There's more." Allen said confusedly.

There appeared to be a trail of the same candy that led into the cornfield.

"Let's follow." Ben said.
"No! You heard the story." Sally said quickly.
"Oh come on! Do you really believe that?" Ben asked.

The children looked at each other as if what to do.

"I'll go." Ben said.
"Me too…" Frank said followed by Sarah and Allen.

Everyone began volunteering.

"Fine, but stay close." Sally said.

The children crept into the cornfield slowly. About halfway through, SNAP!

"What was that?" Frank asked.

Jumping backwards, everyone began screaming.

"STOP!" shouted Allen.

Silence once again.

"It was probably an animal that we scared away now." Allen said.
"Let's keep moving." Sarah said.

They continued to follow the candy trail.

"Where do you think it leads?" Sally asked.
"I don't know." Ben said.

A little more into the field, they began to hear whispers.

"Do you hear that?" Frank asked.
"Shush!" Allen loudly whispered.

They all inched a little closer to the whispering sounds. The whispers suddenly stopped. They hovered close to each other in silence, afraid to move. Staring through the corn, they tried to see what was ahead. Suddenly, the sounds of corn popping became loud. Popping was all around them.

"Run!" Shouted Frank.

They took off running as fast as their little legs would let them.

"I hear it coming closer!" Sarah shouted.
"Keep running!" Frank hollered.
"It's going to kill us!" Sally cried out.
"Run faster!" Allen exclaimed.

They finally reached the exit of the cornfield. Stumbling over on top of each other, they tried to catch their breaths.

"What was that?" Sally asked.
"Where did it go?" Frank asked.
"Listen!" Ben whispered loudly.

As they sat in fear, there was no sound other than the wind softly blowing.

"I want to go home." Sarah said.
"Come on." Allen said as he helped everyone off the ground.

Beginning to walk away, they heard another corn crack behind them.

"Not again!"
"Just move quickly. Don't stop."

They scurried back in a hurry. They were all relieved to have made it safely.

"Where have you all been?" Timothy asked.
"Out playing." Sarah said.
"You look like you guys have seen a ghost. Wait, you went to the cornfield, didn't you?" asked Timothy.
"Yes, but don't tell mom." Sarah said.
"I'm surprised you made it back alive." Timothy said.
"Well, we almost didn't." Sally said.
"Yeah whatever was chasing us, almost got us." Frank claimed.

They all decided they would never return to the forbidden cornfield again.

SPOOKY WOODS

Isaac and Stacy went to visit their grandparents a few hours away. A set of woods on the edge of town caught the eyes of Stacy. She overheard conversations of the eerie feelings it gave if anyone who dared to go near the woods. It felt like a rash of bumps all over your body. Every hair stood up on your arms.

"What was it about these woods that had such power to give fear?" Stacy questioned.

Stacy was out playing with the neighborhood kids one day.

"Let's play hide and go seek in the spooky woods." Sam suggested.
"Are you crazy?" Stacy asked.
"I'll go in if you do." Thomas said.
"No way." Stacy said.
"What could happen?" Sam asked sarcastically.
"It's almost dark." Angel said.
"So what." Thomas said.
"No one ever enters those woods." Angel stated.
"Let's go home." Stacy said.
"Chicken." Sam said.

They left and returned home before dinner. While eating,

"Grandma, how come no one likes the woods at the edge of town?" Stacy asked.
"Stay away from that area." Grandma said.
"But why?" Stacy asked in curiosity.

"No one has been in them woods for decades. A man use to live there. He had a nice little cabin at one time until he was murdered. The cabin has been abandoned since. It still sits back in the woods. Nobody ever goes there." Grandma explained.

After dinner, Stacy and Issac headed to bed.

"Do you believe that story?" Sarah asked her brother.
"Grandpa says it's true, and that the man's ghost haunts the woods." Isaac replied as he went to bed.

The next day Stacy went out to play again. She kept thinking about the story of the murdered man.

"Why do you keep staring down the road?" Angel asked.
"Do you know about the story of the old man?" Stacy asked.
"You mean the murder?" Sam asked.
"Yes." Stacy replied.
"Our parents told us a long time ago. The whole town knows. They never found who did it." Thomas said.
"We should go check out his cabin." Sam stated.
"No one is allowed in those woods." Angel said.
"Who's going to find out?" Sam asked.
"Nothing has happened since then." Thomas said.

The four of them decided to walk to the woods and enter.

"How far is the cabin?" Stacy asked.
"I heard it sits by a stream." Angel replied.

After awhile of walking, they began hearing running water.

"It's this way!" Thomas exclaimed.

They eventually came upon a little stream in the woods.

"Where is the cabin?" Stacy asked.
"Look! It's over there." Sam said pointing to the other side of the creek.

They approached the cabin slowly.

"Are you going to go in?" Angel asked.
"I will go in." Thomas replied.

Reaching the steps of the cabin,

"Is that blood?" Sam asked.
"Okay, I'm not going in." Angel said.
"Oh stop, Let's keep going." Thomas said.

Every step creaked. The whole cabin had grown weak over time. Finally reaching the door, they slowly pushed it open.

"What if his dead body is still in there?" Stacy asked.
"He was buried." Thomas replied.
"Maybe we shouldn't go in." Angel stated.
"I will go first." Sam said.

The rest followed behind. Their hearts racing in fear. All of a sudden, CRASH!

"What was that?" Stacy asked.

"HELP!" Yelled a voice.

Angel had fallen through the floor.

"Help her!" Stacy shouted.

They pulled her out quickly.

"We need to get out of here." Sam stated.
"Wait! What was that?" Thomas asked.

The sounds of light tapping began.

"Where is it coming from?" Angel asked.
"It's the dead man!" They all screamed. Stacy whispered loudly.
"I think it's coming from the bedroom." Sam said.

They crept over to the bedroom in fear of what secret the bedroom held. Thomas pushed the bedroom door open quickly. Blood stains ran down the walls. The bed torn apart as if there were some kind of struggle. Blood dried sheets and pillows thrown across the floor.

"I'm not going in there." Stacy stated.
"I'm not either." Angel said.
"We should leave." Sam said.

A dark shadow suddenly traveled along the side of one wall. They all took off running and screaming out of the cabin back into the woods.

"It's the dead man!"

After crossing the stream, they stopped to catch their breaths.

"Do you think it was his ghost?" Stacy asked.

SNAP! The breaking sounds of tree limbs seemed to be coming towards them.

"Run!" Thomas shouted.
"The dead man is going to kill us!" Angel screamed.

They ran until they arrived back to the street leading to town. Out of breath,

"Is he still coming?" Stacy asked.
"No, I think we are safe now." Angel replied.
"I'm never going back in them woods again." Sam stated.
"Come on, Let's go home." Thomas said.

After Stacy's parents returned to pick her and Isaac up,

"Did you have fun at Grandma's?"

Stacy nodded and remained quiet for the car ride home. She kept the secret of venturing through the woods to herself, never to speak about it again.

HAUNTED HOUSE

Standing in line, she shivered. The wind was cool, the night dark. Staring next door, it was a scary house full of cobwebs in the windows. Inside was like the midnight sky. Nothing could be seen from afar. A few windows had been boarded up and spray painted black. Cracks lined in various sections of the outside walls. An old chimney was full of bats flying out.

Some say if you pass the house in the dark, shadows can be seen walking back and forth in front of the windows. The street lights shine just bright enough to see the motions of ghosts if you are close.

It was Halloween night. All the children were out collecting candy around the neighborhood. Nobody dared to walk into the yard of the true haunted house. The children stood in line at each house surrounding the spooky one. Waiting to receive a handful of candy.

"I dare you to go knock on that door." Liam said as he pointed to the house next door.

"No." Hannah replied shaking.

She was visiting cousins for the holiday.

"Are you scared?" Liam asked.
"Yes." Hannah replied.
"It's just an old abandoned house." Liam stated.
"Then you go." Hannah said.
"I heard if you knock on the door then the house will eat you." Billy said.
"That's not true." Liam said.
"Then go knock on the door and find out." Hannah suggested.

"Why don't you knock?" Liam asked.
"It was your idea." Hannah replied.
"I'm not going to volunteer." Billy said.
"Me either." Hannah said.

They received their candy and proceeded past the scary house. Liam noticed the streets were getting bare.

"Everyone is going inside their houses now." Liam said.
"I guess Halloween is over." Billy said.
"I'm going home. It's getting late." Hannah said.
"Wait!" Liam whispered loudly.

Hannah turned around in curiosity.

"Did you see the shadows?" Liam asked.
"No." Billy replied.
"I don't see anything. It's dark in there." Hannah said.
"If we move closer, we can see inside the windows." Liam stated.
"I don't want to. It's creepy at that house." Hannah said.
"It's not creepy." Liam said.
"It looks scary from here." Billy said.
"Oh come on!" Liam said as he grabbed Hannah's hand.

He pulled Hannah onto the front yard of the scary house. At the same time, Billy followed close behind slightly holding on to Hannah's shirt. As they approached near the house, the wind picked up.

"I think it might rain." Hannah said.

Dark clouds began hovering over the scary house. Branches were breaking from the naked trees. Then, it happened. The street lights hit the windows just enough for the shadows to appear.

"I'm scared." Hannah said.
"You see the shadows now?" Liam asked.
"Yes." Hannah replied.
"Wait a minute. There's an old man in that house." Billy said.
"Can I help you?" A strange voice suddenly asked.
"Ahh!" They all screamed at once.

The children turned quickly to the voice. There was a crippled man standing with a cane.

"Why are you peeping in my windows?" The man asked.
"You live here?" Billy asked.
"Yes." The man replied.
"Who is the old man?" Hannah asked.
"That is my father." The man replied.
"How come we have never seen you around?" Liam asked.
"We are not welcome by many people around here. Therefore, we don't go out much." The man replied.
"I always thought this place was haunted and abandoned. I've never seen anyone over here." Billy said.
"Well, it's not." The man said.
"We will leave now." Hannah said as she turned to walk away.
"Wait." The man said.

They turned to the man once again.

"It's Halloween. I don't have much, but I think I have a few pieces of candy." The man said.

"No thank you. We have plenty in our buckets." Billy said.

The man stood staring at the three of us.

"Be on your way then." The man said as he walked away.

They hurried down the road away from the house.

"See, nothing to be scared about." Liam said.
"Oh, you were scared." Billy said.
"We all were." Hannah said.
"Well, at least we don't have to be scared anymore. They don't seem like bad people." Billy said.

Hannah stopped for a moment.

"Maybe others should know about them." Hannah said.
"Why?" Liam asked.
"Then they can start coming out more." Hannah replied.
"Yeah, I'm sure his father is friendly too." Billy said.

They continued walking.

"They seem harmless." Hannah said.
"I'm sure they do get lonely in there." Liam said.
"I would be lonely sitting in a house all the time. Never having anyone to talk to." Hannah said.
"Maybe at the next neighborhood cookout we could get our parents to invite them." Billy suggested.
"Maybe." Liam said.

The children eventually arrived home.

"Where have you been?" Aunt asked.
"We was out walking around." Liam replied.
"No more exploring tonight. Hit the bed." Aunt said.

They started to go to bed when Hannah became curious.

"Aunt, do you know the people that live in the scary house across town?" Hannah asked.
"Yes, actually I see them around sometimes." Aunt replied.
"How come no one likes them?" Hannah asked.
"Them? You talked to them?" Aunt asked.
"Well, yeah." Hannah replied.
"Oh child, you stay away from them." Aunt said.
"Why?" Hannah asked.

Aunt looked at the children.

"A long time ago, on Halloween night, it has been said that the father killed a child for asking for candy. It was never proven, but the town knew who did it. The town stopped talking to them after that." Aunt explained.
"But what if they didn't do it?" Hannah asked.
"He did. No more discussing it. You all stay away from that house." Aunt stated.
"Okay." They all said.

Aunt was pretty sure of herself. The children went off to bed thinking about how they trespassed onto the spooky property. Either they were lucky to not get hurt by the man or the story wasn't true. With the case going unsolved, they wouldn't know it to be true or not.

THE ATTIC

It was a scary place to be in. The darkness surrounded them everywhere they looked. Little windows provided no help to their vision.

"How are we going to get out of here?" Karen asked.
"The windows are too small to fit through." Maria said.

Karen was at a sleepover at a friend's house. They felt around as if they were blind trying to find any way out.

"We will be stuck in here forever." Jessica said.
"Calm down. We will get out." Brittany stated.

They began tripping over objects around them.

"Be careful." Maria said.
"I can't see anything." Jessica said.

About that time, a light shined across the room.

"What is that?" Brittany asked.

They made their way towards the light coming in from a small locked window.

"Look! It's headlights." Karen excitedly said.
"Someone is here." Maria said.

They began banging on the window with their hands.

"HELP!" They all shouted.

Yelling out didn't save them. The windows were sound proof. The car eventually left.

"We are never getting out of here." Karen said.
"We will find a way." Brittany said.

They sat together thinking of ways to escape. BANG! A loud noise came out of nowhere. They all screamed as they hovered in a corner. The girls were frightened.

"What was that?" Karen asked.
"I don't know." Jessica replied.
"I'm not going to find out." Maria said.

They continued to hover over top of each other scared like little mice. The girls were confused as to what was causing the noises.

"This is crazy!" Brittany claimed.
"There has to be another way out of here." Maria said.
"Hush! I hear footsteps." Jessica said.

They listened closely to the sounds of steps lightly shuffling across the floor.

"I think it's coming this way." Karen said.
"Maybe it's a ghost." Jessica said.
"I don't believe in ghosts." Brittany said.

"They are real, just like you and me." Jessica said.
"Maybe it wants to turn us into ghosts." Maria said.
"Stop it already. No ghosts are going to kill us." Brittany said.

A few seconds later,

"Hello!" Karen loudly whispered.

No response answered back.

"Is anyone there?" Brittany whispered out.

Still no response. The sounds of footsteps picked back up. It was a little louder this time.

"It must be the woman who died in this house." Jessica said.
"What do you mean?" Karen asked.
"A long time ago a woman hung herself here." Jessica replied.
"This is a joke." Brittany said.
"No, my grandma told me about it." Jessica said.
"Why did she hang herself?" Maria asked.
"She was depressed over her boyfriend. She was a friend of my grandma. She hung herself in this attic. It was days before anyone found her." Jessica explained.

The girls held tight to each other's clothes.

"We should run." Jessica said.
"Where would we run to?" Brittany asked.

After a few moments of shaking in a corner, a light appeared from the floor in the middle of the room. Someone opened the attic door. The ladder dropped as they ran over. They were excited to be getting out of the scary attic.

"We're saved!" Karen hollered out.

They all began climbing down the ladder.

"What are you doing up there?" Mom asked.
"We got trapped." Brittany replied.
"Who shut the door anyway?" Jessica asked.
"The ghost." Maria replied.

Mom stared at the girls for a moment. She couldn't believe what she was hearing.

"There isn't a ghost. Sometimes you have to be careful with ladder doors. They can shut on their own." Mom explained.

The girls looked at each other. They didn't want to talk about the woman who hung herself.

"I thought we would die up there!" Jessica said.

They turned back to mom.

"How did you know we were up there anyway?" Brittany asked.
"I came home, couldn't find anyone, so I decided to look upstairs after hearing noises." Mom replied.

The girls looked at each other.

"We are glad you did." Maria said.
"Yeah we would have been up there forever." Karen said.
"We would of eventually been found." Maria said.
"Yeah like the woman was found." Jessica said.
"What woman?" Mom asked.
"Nothing. Just some story." Brittany replied.

Mom began to walk away.

"Come get something to eat." Mom said.

They ate and felt better. It was time for bed.

"Well, that was a scary adventure." Karen said.
"Yes it was." Maria said.
"We won't be doing that again." Jessica said.
"Your the one that wanted to go up." Brittany said.
"I didn't think we would get stuck." Jessica said.
"I doesn't matter now. We are out of there and safe. We won't go back up there." Maria said.
"Do you really believe the woman's ghost would still be in the attic of the house?" Karen asked.
"We can talk about that another time." Jessica said.
"Yeah, we should get some sleep." Brittany said.

They all went to bed, never to go near the attic again.

GRAVEYARD HUNT

A dark place to play in, everyone knew the stories behind the graveyard. The fascination of them overpowered the need to stay away. Once darkness fell, the children found themselves involved with something unexpected when they went against rules and played in an area they shouldn't have. They stayed in a hotel for the weekend with their parents, which was located next to a graveyard.

It wasn't an ordinary graveyard. This was an old one with broken stoned heads on each site. No one visited or used the yard for burial anymore. Some of the stones were big enough to stand behind. The dark woods surrounded three sides of the yard with a small fence that was falling apart.

"Let's go walk the yard." Brian said.
"It's going to be dark soon." Sue said.
"We should just stay at the hotel." Toby said.
"That would be a good idea." Sue said.

They began to walk away.

"You're not scared, are you?" Brian asked.
"Maybe I am." Sue replied.
"It's been said that the ghosts of the old graveyard haunt the hotel at night." Brian explained.
"No they don't." Sue said.
"You will find out tonight when you are sleeping." Brian said.
"You just want to scare me." Sue said.

Sue went into her brother's arms.

"Don't scare her." Toby said.
"You want to walk the yard?" Devon asked.
"I'm not scared. Come on." Brian replied.
"I will too." Toby said.
"Then let's go." Devon said.

The children went out behind the hotel to the graveyard.

"It's almost dark." Sue said.
"It's fine. We won't be long." Toby said.
"See there's nothing spooky about this yard." Devon said.
"I dare you all to go hide behind a stone. I will come find you." Brian said.
"We shouldn't bother the dead." Toby said.
"We are not disturbing anyone. Just hiding. It's harmless play." Brian said.
"Come on Sue. What do you say?" Devon asked.

Sue stood with confidence that her cousin was only out to scare her. She would do the hide.

"I will. You can't scare me." Sue said.

They all ran to hide behind a stone deep within the yard. It had seemed like forever that Sue was standing behind one of the bigger stones. At this point, darkness had fallen. As Sue stood glancing around her, she could see the night getting thick. Fog began through the yard. The wind had a chill to it.

"Had everyone forgotten about me?'" Sue quietly asked herself.

She was frightened while noises and whispers began around her. Then, it became silent.

"Toby." Sue whispered out.

No answer. She wasn't sure what to do. No one was in sight. Everyone left her alone in the graveyard. Out of nowhere, slight crying sounds came through the wind. Shivering and scared, Sue decided to take a chance and run out of the graveyard.

As she stepped from behind her big stone, Sue seen shadows of people walking around. She assumed it was probably her family. Being a little scared, she wanted to find her brother.

"Toby!" Sue whispered loudly.

But it wasn't her brother. Dark shadows slowly approached the stone Sue was standing by. She became even more frightened. Sue took off running toward the entrance of the graveyard while screaming.

"HELP!" Sue yelled out.

All the way out of the yard she screamed and ran. As she exited the graveyard, her brother and other family surrounded her.

"Are you okay?" Toby asked.

Sue fell to the ground trying to catch her breath.

"Why did you leave me in there?" Sue asked.
"You wasn't scared was you?" Brian asked.
"That wasn't a funny joke." Toby said.

Toby helped Sue off the ground.

"You came running out too." Devon said.
"Yeah but I thought she was out here already." Toby said.

They stood arguing in front of the graveyard.

"Why did you all leave?" Sue asked.
"The dark shadows were trying to get us, so we ran out. I didn't want to stay in there." Devon said.
"I seen them too." Sue said.
"Let's get back to our rooms." Toby suggested.

They began to walk away.

"Don't you want to play with the shadows more? Are you all too scared?" Brian asked.

Toby turned around.

"Are you serious?" Toby asked.
"They won't hurt you." Brian said.
"I'm taking my sister back to her room." Toby said.

Suddenly, the children heard loud growling sounds.

"What was that?" Devon asked.
"The dark shadows are coming!" Sue exclaimed.
"Run for your life!" Toby shouted.

They all ran into the hotel lobby.

"Whoa! Slow down." A worker said.

Sue grabbed a hold of the worker's clothing.

"The dark shadows were trying to get us. You have to save us from them." Sue claimed.

The worker looked at them strangely. He knew the children had probably been out to the graveyard.

"Why are you out of your rooms?" The worker asked.
"We were exploring the yards." Devon replied.
"You shouldn't be out in the yards this late. The dark shadows have been known to protect their home." The worker explained.

The children looked scared.

"What do you mean?" Sue asked.
"Just stay in your rooms tonight." The worker said firmly.
"Okay we will." Devon said.

The children returned to their rooms for the rest of the night. The next morning, they parted their ways home, never telling their parents about the graveyard adventure.

ABANDONED MANSION

The rooms were dark and moist. The air cold and breezy. Coffins lined the walls of each room. Old wooden coffins with lids that barely covered them. It was a scary place to be. Sky and Ty ventured too far with neighborhood kids.

They came across an abandoned building the next town over. Bricks lay on the ground where they had fallen from the sides of the building. The children made the brave decision to go in and explore. An hour before, a man they met in the park had told them a story about this old building.

"I'm bored." Michael said.
"Wish there was something scary to do." Chris said.
"Yeah, it is getting close to full moon night." Ty said.
"I don't think there is much to do around here that is scary." Megan said.
"There has to be something." Sky said.

As they sat around discussing things to do,

"Your looking for something scary?" A man asked.

They turned around quickly.

"Who are you?" Sky asked.
"There's an abandoned mansion in the next town over. If you hurry, you will make it there before dark." The man said.

They looked at each other in confusion.

"What is so scary about that?" Michael asked.

"Dead bodies wrapped in tight sheets are still inside. They call them mummies. Be careful not to disturb them though." The man explained.

The man now had the children's attention.

"What happens if you do?" Megan asked.
"They will turn you into a mummy." The man said.

Everyone began to laugh sarcastically.

"I don't believe you." Chris said.
"Go find out for yourself." The man said.
"Maybe we will." Michael said.

The children decided to hike to the next town until they reached the old building.

"It does look scary." Sky said.
"What if the guy was telling the truth? There could be a building full of mummies." Megan asked.

They wasn't sure whether to go inside.

"Do you really think there would be mummies inside? Who would store mummies?" Michael asked.
"There's only one way to find out." Ty said.

A short time passed before the children went inside the old building. They walked close to stay together. After a few moments of exploring, KNOCK, KNOCK, Knock...

"Someone is here." Chris said.
"Did you hear the knocking?" Megan asked.
"Where is it coming from?" Sky asked.
"Yes, sounds like this way." Ty said.

They followed the knocking sounds to a room in the basement of the mansion.

"AHHH!" Sky screamed.

Everyone jumped backwards looking around them. Scared, they wasn't sure what she was screaming about.

"What?" Michael asked.
"Mice!" Megan shouted.
"Come this way." Ty said.
"Watch where you're stepping." Chris said.

A group of mice ran around them as if they were running from something.

"Maybe we should run too." Sky suggested.
"Nonsense! Come on, stay close." Ty said.
"This place is scary and smelly." Megan said.

The children continued into the basement room. The knocking got louder.

"I'm scared." Sky said.

"You will be fine." Ty said.
"The knocking is coming from one of these coffins." Michael said.
"We need to figure out which one." Chris said.
"What if there are mummies in all of them?" Megan asked.

Ty stood shaking his head.

"There are no mummies here." Ty said.

They glanced around trying to figure out which direction to go. The children had to find where the knocking was coming from.

"Should we open them all?" Chris asked.
"No, keep following the knock. This way." Ty replied.

The knocking stopped once they approached a small coffin in the middle of the room.

"It's small." Megan said.
"Maybe a child is in there." Sky said.
"Or a midget mummy." Chris said.

They stood in silence for a moment. Then, a light tap on the coffin. It startled them.

"Open it." Michael said.
"No, you open it." Chris said.
"I'm not going to open it." Megan said.
"Fine, I will." Ty said.

He slowly approached the coffin lid with his hand.

"What are you waiting on?" Michael asked.
"Just hush. I'm going to open it." Ty replied.
"Be careful. These coffins look old." Sky said.

As he began to put his hand on the coffin, the lid flew open quickly. A mummy sat up to reach for him.

"Mummies!" Sky screamed.
"Run!" Ty shouted.

They began to run out of the room, tripping and knocking over coffins along the way.

"Mummies are everywhere!" Chris hollered.
"We are going to be turned into mummies! Let's get out of here!" Sky screamed.
"How do we get out of here?" Megan asked.
"This way!" Ty hollered.

They made it out safely and ran straight home.

"We let all the mummies out." Sky said.
"What are we going to do?" Megan asked.
"Nothing. I'm sure someone was probably just playing a joke on us." Ty replied.

They sat to calm down for a few moments.

"Yeah, the man at the park was probably behind it all." Chris claimed.
"Well, he did tell us where to go." Michael said.

"Don't tell anyone what happened." Ty suggested.
"We would be in trouble." Michael said.
"Just keep the secret among us. Let's go to bed." Ty said.

They swore to secrecy and to never go back to the mansion again.

BAT CAVE

Legend has it, there was a cave on the east side of the mountain that a serial killer once used to hide his victims. Bats would come in at night and feed off of the decomposing bodies. Those who can find the cave and enter, will see fragments of the victim's bones throughout. This is a tale that had been told for generations.

How true is this story?

Sophia was invited to go on a cabin trip with her friend and parents. It was fun for the first few days until they made friends with other camper's children. Then, the real fun began. Everyone was aware of the stories of the serial killer except the new comers. When made aware, Sophia wanted to go home.

"It's just on the other side of that hill over there. Come on." Jefferey said.
"I don't want go." Sophia said.
"Stop being a baby." Mark said.

The four kept walking.

"Our parents will be looking for us soon." Heather claimed.
"We will be back before dark." Jeffrey said.

Sophia grew concerned.

"What if the serial killer is still alive." Sophia asked.
"They executed him for the killings." Mark replied.

This didn't help Sophia any.

"Come on. It has to be here behind these tree branches. Help me move them." Jeffrey said.

They all began moving branches away from an opening in the hillside.

"This is it!" Mark exclaimed.
"I don't want to go in." Sophia said.
"There's nothing in there anymore." Mark said.

Weird sounds came out of the cave.

"Bats are." Heather said.
"Bats are harmless." Jeffrey stated.

Deciding to go in, they crawled on their knees through the hole. Eventually they came to an open area where they could stand. The cave had a small stream running through the middle of it. Walking along the stream of the cave, they began hearing flapping noises.

"What is that?" Sophia asked.

They looked above to see tiny black creatures flying around making little squeaking noises.

"BATS!" Heather screamed.

About that time, Sophia slipped down a slight muddy slope into the water. Everyone pulled her out. Her clothes were wet and muddy.

The group continued to walk along the stream of water hoping to find a way out of the cave.

"Cover your heads and move fast." Jeffrey said.
"There has to be an exit soon." Mark said.

They walked and walked. There was no exit.

"Maybe we should turn around and go back to the entrance." Heather suggested.
"I'm not going back through all them bats." Jeffrey said.
"They will eat us!" Sophia exclaimed.

Walking a little further,

"What is this?" Heather asked.

Heather bent down to explore the dirt. She admired little white hard fragments all over the ground.

"These are tiny fragments of bones. I'm not sure where they would come from." Mark said.
"The bones of the dead victims!" Sophia said.

The children became scared.

"Don't touch them." Jefferey said.
"Let's keep moving forward." Mark said.

They continued to walk hand in hand. They came upon a small mud hill.

"What is this?" Sophia asked.

After observing,

"Maybe we should climb up it." Heather said.
"I see a small light from above." Sophia said.

Looking over the muddy hill,

"The exit must be over this mud hill. It's the only way out most likely." Heather said.
"Let's climb it and see." Mark said.

Everyone took turns climbing the small mud hill. When it came to Sophia's turn, she couldn't climb it alone. Her clothes were still wet from where she had fallen into the stream, which made her slide back down the hill. The hill was slippery.

"Push her up from the bottom and we will pull her up from the top." Jeffrey said.

They all helped push or pull. Eventually, Sophia made it to the top of the mud hill.

"Now everyone else climb up." Mark said.

After everyone was up, they crawled through another hole together.

"I see the outside." Heather said.
"We are saved!" Sophia said.

They stopped for a moment to look.

"Yes, it's an exit!" Mark said.
"Go, hurry, get out of here." Jeffrey said.

They climbed out of the cave.

"I'm leaving." Sophia said.

After getting back, they cleaned up.

"Why are you all so dirty?" Mom asked.
"We were playing by a creek we found. It was wet and muddy." Heather replied.
"Get cleaned up and come inside for dinner. It is getting late." Mom said.

The children cleaned up an ate. Before bed,

"I won't do that again." Sophia said.
"Do you think those were real bones?" Heather asked.
"Yes, bones of animals most likely." Mark said.

The children kept their adventure in the bat cave quiet and went about their night. They wanted to forget about almost getting eaten by bats.

CREEPY ROAD

"Where are you off to?" Sierra asked.
"I'm sneaking out tonight." Tony replied.

Sierra looked at Tony with confusion. He had never left the house at night before that she was aware of.

"You will get in trouble." Sierra claimed.
"Not if mom doesn't find out." Tony said.

Sierra now became curious.

"What are you going to be doing?" Sierra asked.
"I'm going out riding around with friends. Don't tell anyone." Tony replied.
"I want to come." Sierra said.

Tony looked at Sierra with confusion this time.

"You should be in bed." Tony stated.
"I can't sleep." Sierra said.

After a few minutes of thinking,

"Hurry, come on, and be quiet." Tony said.

They climbed out the window quietly together. Tony's friends were waiting down the road.

"You had to bring your sister?" Max asked.

"She caught me sneaking out. I'm covering my tracks. She won't be a bother." Tony replied.

Driving down the road,

"So, what is this creepy road your talking about?" Tony asked.

"Creepy road?" Sierra asked.

"Yeah, be quiet and sit back." Tony quietly replied.

"It's a little drive." Max said.

"A girl got slaughtered on the road a long time ago. The guy who cut her up, spread her body pieces up and down the road." Charles explained.

"Yeah, she can be seen walking the street trying to find her body." Bobby said.

"Can I go back home?" Sierra asked.

"Too late now." Max said.

They finally get to the road.

"Here it is." Charles said.

Slowly driving down the road,

"Look! There's the old tree." Bobby said.

"It has no leaves." Sierra said.

"The girl was killed under that tree." Bobby said.

"Leaves haven't grown on that tree since her death." Max said.

"The girl should be here somewhere." Charles said.

They glanced around them.

"This is giving me chills." Tony said.
"You're not scared are you?" Max asked.

At the end of the road,

"I didn't see her." Bobby said.
"Let's turn around." Max said.

The road was surrounded by high fields of grass and trees. After turning around in a ditch, they headed back up the road. Suddenly they approached what looked like an animal on the ground in the middle of the road.

"What kind of animal is that?" Sierra asked.
"It looks like a deer." Tony replied.
"Why would a deer be laying dead in the middle of the road?" Sierra asked.

They all stared at each other in confusion.

"Wait, that wasn't there on the way down the road." Charles stated.
"What is going on?" Bobby asked.
"Someone might be trying to lure us out of the car. Don't trust it." Tony replied.

Sierra became scared.

"I'm not getting out to move the deer." Charles said.
"We could be slaughtered to death." Bobby said.

Frightened, Sierra grabbed her brother by the arm.
"I want go home now." Sierra said.
"I'm going around it. Hold on!" Bobby said.

Bobby stomped on the gas and swerved around the animal without stopping.

"Ahhh!!" They all screamed.

He suddenly stomped on the brakes.

"Is everyone okay?" Bobby asked.
"Yes, but where did the animal go?" Tony asked.

Everyone looked around.

"I have no idea." Charles replied.
"It was just there." Max said.
"We need to get out of here." Tony said.

As they began to drive off, Bobby slammed on his brakes once again. He noticed something.

"What is that?" Bobby asked.

Everyone's eyes were on the front of the car.

"It's the girl." Charles said.
"I'm scared." Sierra said.
"Hide your eyes." Tony said.

Sierra put her head on Tony's shirt.

"What is she doing?" Bobby asked.
"She's looking for her body parts." Max replied.

All of a sudden, the ghost woman looked up at the car. Her eyes were fixated on the boys.

"She's looking at us." Charles said.
"She's going to kill us." Max said.
"No she's not." Bobby said.

After a few moments,

"She's walking over here!" Tony shouted.
"Go, go, go!" Charles hollered.
"Go now!" Max screamed.

Bobby floored the gas once again. Sierra snuggled to her brother crying. Charles, Max, and Tony shouted.
Once off the road, Bobby found a gas station and pulled over.

"Did she follow us?" Bobby asked.

They all glanced around the outside of the car.

"I don't think so." Charles replied.

Everyone gave a sigh of relief.

"Let's go home." Bobby said.

Bobby dropped everyone off and went home himself. Tony and Sierra never went back to the creepy road again.

LAKE DOCK

During a vacation, Stella and Travis visited a small lake with an old dock often. Other children played around the dock also. One evening after dinner, they decided to go meet others at the dock again. They made quite a few friends while vacationing.

"Don't forget, this is our last night here." Mom stated.
"Yes, we are going to play with our friends one last time and say our goodbyes." Travis explained.

Mom glanced at the two standing at the door.

"Have fun, and stay out of the lake." Mom said.
"We will." Travis said.

They ran out to the dock to meet the other children. They were excited to spend one more night chilling with the friends they made.

"It's a full moon tonight." James said.
"I know, scary." Stella said.

Staring at the moon,

"I've heard a lot can happen on full moons." Natalie said.
"Full moon stories are just myths." Zachary said.

Zachary began to giggle.

"Not all of them." Travis claimed.

The children began sitting around on the dock.

"I dare you to jump in." Bridget said.

Natalie looked at Bridget.

"You first." Natalie said.
"We are not supposed to be in the water." Stella said.

James decided to join the conversation.

"Who's going to find out?" James asked.
"I'm not jumping in." Stella said.
"What are you scared of?" James asked.

Stella shrugged her shoulders at James. She knew it wouldn't be her going into the water.

"I'll jump in if you do." Zachary said.
"I don't want to jump in." Travis said.

After a few minutes, they began to hear splashing from under them.

"Someone is under the dock." Stella said.

They began moving around.

"It's just someone trying to scare us." Bridget claimed.

Again, more splashing.

"Okay, who is under there?" Zachary asked.
"We are all here." Travis said.

An old man approached.

"That would be my brother." The man stated.

Everyone turned to look at the strange man. They wasn't sure if he was telling the truth.

"Well tell him to stop." Zachary said.
"He's dead." The man said.

They stared at the old man.

"He got sucked under the water years ago. He was told to stay out of the water, but he wouldn't listen." The man explained.

The children looked at each other.

"See, and you wanted to jump in. You would have been drowned by the boy." Stella said.
"I come back every full moon to hear him splashing around." The man said.

They turned back to the man.

"It's his ghost in the water?" Natalie asked.
"Yes." The man replied.

Frightened, the children became quiet. The man's story had

frightened them a little.

"No one is allowed to swim in the lake." The man said.
"I'm not jumping in and being sucked under." Stella said.
"You shouldn't even be on the dock." The man said.

They grew curious.

"Why?" Natalie asked.
"Sometimes my brother can get playful and pull little kids in from the dock." The man replied.

Freaked out by the old man's story, the children jumped up and ran off the dock.

"Well, I must be going now." The man said.

The man walked away slowly.

"Do you believe it's true?" Natalie asked.
"You heard the splashes." Travis replied.
"Could of been a fish." James said.
"No fish is going to splash like that." Bridget said.

Standing around discussing what it could be, moments later,

"SPLASH!"

The children turned quickly towards the water.

"It's him again!" Travis yelled out.

All of a sudden, the ghost of a little boy comes walking slowly out of the lake.

"I told you it wasn't a fish!" Bridget yelled.

They became frightened as the boy continued to walk towards them.

"RUN!" James shouted.

Everyone ran to one of the cabins.

"Is he still coming?" Stella asked.
"I don't see him." Travis replied.

The children stood looking out into the darkness. They were happy that the little boy went away.

"Well, that was an exciting last night together. Something to remember." James stated.
"We was out there last night and didn't see him." Natalie said.
"Remember, the man said he only comes on full moon nights." Bridget said.
"We better go in now." Travis suggested.
"Yeah it's getting late." Stella said.

Everyone said their goodbyes and good nights. Then, back to their cabins to sleep. The next morning, everyone went home. No one told their parents about the little boy in the water.

BASEMENT SHADOWS

Elizabeth decided to stay at her friend, Valerie's, house for a night. They enjoyed an evening of popcorn and movies. It was late when the movies were over, so the two of them decided to go to bed.

In the middle of the night, Elizabeth went to the kitchen to get a drink of water. All of a sudden, she heard noises coming from the basement. She slowly made her way to the door. After opening it, she decided to walk down the steps. Each step she took, the stairs creaked.

"Maybe I shouldn't be going down here. I should be in bed." Elizabeth said to herself.

The closer she got to the basement, the more the air had an eerie chill to it. It was dark and smelt musty. Maybe due to some water pipe leakage. Small windows let little moon light in. She could barely see her hands in front of her face.

The basement didn't seem like a good place to be in. As she reached the bottom, the door at the top of the steps closed. Shivering in fear, Elizabeth stood frozen in the moment.

"Why did the door close?" Elizabeth asked herself.

"What should I do?" Elizabeth continued to question.

Suddenly, a voice came out of the darkness.

"What are you doing out of bed?" A boy asked.

Elizabeth screamed.

"Hush! It's just me." The boy said.

Valerie's brother, Raymond, grabbed Elizabeth to hush her up.

"You scared me." Elizabeth said.

Elizabeth stood trying to catch her breath.

"What are you doing down here?" Elizabeth asked.
"I come down here to listen for ghosts at night." Raymond replied.

She looked at Raymond with confusion. Elizabeth didn't want to believe in ghosts.

"Ghosts?" Elizabeth asked.
"Yes, do you want to try?" Raymond asked.

Elizabeth became hesitant.

"I don't know." Elizabeth replied.
"Come on, sit here with me." Raymond said.

They sat down in the middle of the room. Elizabeth was unsure whether to continue.

"Close your eyes and listen." Raymond said.
"Listen for what?" Elizabeth asked.
"The ghosts." Raymond replied.

The two sat for a few more moments. Then, they heard shuffling noises from the other side of the room.

"What was that?" Elizabeth asked.

After the noises, Elizabeth became more scared.

"Don't be scared." Raymond replied.

Elizabeth glanced across the room to see shadows moving along the walls. Her heart raced in fear as she shook. The shadows were darker than the darkness itself.

"It's just the family that lived here a long time ago." Raymond explained.

Raymond had arose Sarah's curiosity.

"How do you know this?" Elizabeth asked.
"Research. The father killed them all off one by one, and then turned the gun on himself." Raymond replied.

Elizabeth couldn't believe what she was hearing. Raymond had done a lot of research on this story.

"It was the biggest murder suicide in the area. That was decades ago." Raymond said.

Still curious, Elizabeth continued to listen.

"Sometimes the father ghosts gets upset and tries to come after me, but I get away from him." Raymond continued.

The shadows began hovering towards them. Elizabeth lightly

screamed trying to cover her eyes. Raymond could see that Elizabeth was too frightened, so he grabbed her hand and pulled her upstairs. Elizabeth looked behind her to see the shadow figure following.

"Open the door!" Elizabeth screamed.

Raymond tried turning the knob.

"I'm trying!" Raymond hollered.

The shadow was coming up the stairs slowly. Elizabeth grew even more frightened.

"It's coming! Open the door!" Elizabeth shouted.

Finally, the door opened.

"Go before it gets me!" Elizabeth hollered as she pushed Raymond forward.

Elizabeth and Raymond fell into the kitchen area slamming the basement door behind them. Neither could believe they almost got attacked by a shadow figure. They sat on the floor until they calmed down.

"Are we still alive?" Elizabeth asked.

Raymond pinched her hard.

"OUCH!" Elizabeth hollered.
"Yes you are still alive." Raymond replied.

With an angry face, she stared at him.

"You didn't have to pinch me that hard." Elizabeth stated.
"Sorry." Raymond said.

She got her drink of water after calming down.

"I'm never doing that again." Elizabeth said.

Both looked at each other.

"Don't tell anyone what we did." Raymond said.

Elizabeth thought Raymond would go back down to the basement. This would not be a good idea.

"You are crazy if you go back down there." Elizabeth said.

Sarcastically, Raymond giggled at her. He thought Elizabeth was a funny girl.

"I won't be going back down tonight." Raymond said.

Elizabeth swore to never tell.

"I'm going to bed." Elizabeth said.

The next morning, Elizabeth got up and left. She never told Valerie or anyone else what had happened.

TREE HOUSE

Walking through some woods one day, Jenny and her friends ran into a big dog.

"Where did that dog come from?" Frances asked.
"I have never seen that dog before." Jenny replied.
"Well, it came from somewhere." Darlene said.

The dog began growling at them.

"I think it's going to attack us." Francis said.

It suddenly lunged towards their direction. The girls were stunned at this happening.

"RUN!" Jenny shouted.

They ran through the woods away from the dog. It chased them until they came upon a tree house.

"Climb the tree!" Darlene said.

Once in the tree house safely, the girls sat to rest. The big dog barked at them from below.

"We will be safe here until the dog leaves." Jenny said.

The tree house was small and old. Pieces of its walls were missing. The ladder to the house was barely hanging to the tree. The girls were lucky to make it up the tree before the dog got to them.

"I wonder who built this house." Francis said.
"I don't know, but it's pretty old." Jenny said.

The girls looked around.

"We could probably fix it up one day for a hide out." Jenny suggested.

Frances wasn't excited about the idea.

"The dog lives out here somewhere." Frances said.
"It would be better to build one in our own backyard." Darlene said.

Darkness began to fall.

"We should be heading back." Jenny said.

The three of them glanced around the outside of the tree house with caution.

"I don't see the dog anymore." Francis said.
"Let's get out of here." Darlene said.

As they started to climb down the tree, they began hearing sticks break in the woods. They were scared so the girls climbed back into the house quietly.

"I think the dog is coming back." Jenny said.

The girls became scared. They peeked out the small window of the tree house.

"I don't see anything." Francis said.
"Me either." Darlene said.

Being too scared to leave, the girls sat quietly and listened. The crackling of sticks was getting louder and closer.

"What do you think it is?" Jenny asked.
"Probably animals." Francis quietly said.

Suddenly, it was silent. The girls weren't sure what to do in the moment.

"Go look." Francis suggested.
"You go look." Jenny responded.
"I'm not looking." Francis said.
"Neither am I." Jenny said.

Darlene became agitated with the two. She was tired of hearing them argue.

"Shhh. I'm trying to hear." Darlene whispered.

They continued to listen.

"I think someone is climbing up to the tree house." Darlene said.
"Maybe it's the dog." Francis said.
"Dogs can't climb trees." Jenny said.

The three girls sat tightly together in a corner of the tree house. All the sudden, a head popped up through the hole opening.

"Ahhh!" The girls scream.

It was an older boy.

"What are you doing in my tree house?"

They took a few seconds to collect their thoughts. They didn't know what to say at first.

"We got chased by a dog and came in here to get away from it." Darlene explained.

The boy looked surprised.

"Charlie boy?" The boy asked.

The girls looked confused.

"Who is Charlie boy?" Jenny asked.

The boy entered the tree house and sat down.

"A long time ago, a deformed boy was abandoned by his own town. He moved out into the woods. This actual tree house he built for himself." The boy explained.

Frightened, the girls continued to listen.

"A stranded puppy came along and he trained it to hunt for food. He was hungry one day and couldn't find food. Then, he seen it." The boy continued.

"Seen what?" Jenny asked.

The boy continued with his story.

"A child." The boy claimed.

The three were scared and shaken.

"He demanded the dog to go kill the child and they ate him. The town's people hunted them down and killed both the boy and his dog. The dogs ghost can be seen at times chasing children through the woods."

Jenny began to cry.

"I want to go home." Jenny said.
"You better get home, before the dog returns." The boy said.

The girls jumped up, exited the tree house, and ran straight home without stopping. They cried all the way back. Jenny had decided after that night, she wasn't going to go vacationing with friends anymore.

A Town's Curse

It was a dark road, surrounded by corn fields. He was afraid to leave his sleeping quarters. With doors locked, he wished that someone would come to his rescue soon. Glancing out into the night, he hoped nothing would come out of the darkness to get him.

Alex was on his way to make a delivery. Trucking was his occupation. Deliveries from state to state kept him running on the road a lot away from his family. One night, his truck had broke down. He had no idea what the night had in store for him.

A few miles back, he had stopped to fuel up. Alex had conversation with other truckers.

"Where are you headed?" Another trucker asked.
"Doomsville to drop and pick up another load." Alex replied.

The trucker stared at him for a moment.

"You don't have much time. You better hurry and get out of there soon." The trucker stated.

He looked at the man in confusion.

"What do you mean?" Alex asked.
"Go do your business and be out of that town by dark." The trucker replied.

Alex became curious.

"Why?" Alex asked.

"No one stays out after dark in that town. That town is cursed." The trucker replied.

Alex laughed.

"It's not funny. You will see." The trucker warned.
"I don't believe in curses." Alex said.

The man shook his head.

"If you stay there, you will." The trucker said.
"What happens after dark?" Alex asked.

The man slowly approached Alex.

"You will die if you can't get away from it." The trucker whispered.

Alex stood in front of the man staring into his eyes. It had seemed the trucker was serious.

"How will I die?" Alex asked.
"It kills in different ways. The town is haunted. You don't want to stay there." The trucker replied.

Staring from one trucker to another,

"It?" Alex asked.
"Yes, it." The trucker replied.

Still confused,

"Who is it?" Alex asked.

"The darkness. Those who are out after nightfall, start disappearing into the darkness. Bad things happen to those who are caught outside in the dark." The trucker replied.

Alex backed up from the man slowly to pay for his gas. He didn't want to believe the man.

"Just remember, get out of there before dark. Take my warnings serious." The trucker warned.

Alex began to walk away.

"And if you break down, lock your doors and stay in your truck." The trucker continued to warn.

Alex shrugged off what the man had warned. He didn't want to believe him.

"A cursed town?" Alex Thought to himself.

He drove down the road towards the next town to make his delivery. He dropped his load and hooked to another.

"I'm surprised to see you here." A worker said.
"What do you mean?" Alex asked.
"Well, we usually can't get a driver to come out this way." The worker said.

He became confused again.

"Why not?" Alex asked.

"This town is cursed. Everyone in town knows to be in by dark. If not, the darkness comes for them." The worker explained.

Alex jumped in his truck. He knew after the second conversation, he needed to get away from this town. Either the town was cursed or the people were crazy. Either way, Alex wasn't staying around to find out.

As darkness began, Alex noticed everyone going inside. Just before he reached outside of town, Alex had a blowout.

"I knew I should have got that tire fixed. Now I will be stuck here." Alex said to himself.

Darkness had completely arrived by the time Alex pulled over. He remembered the story of the town's curse and the warning from the other trucker. Alex instantly locked his doors. As he looked around, he could see nothing but the cornfields that his truck lights shined on.

"This doesn't seem too bad." Alex thought.

Scarecrows hung on crosses out in the middle of the fields. Within a few hours, Alex began hearing light screams coming from the cornfields. Big black crows flew around his truck. A couple of them landed on the front of his truck staring at him through the front window. They were dirty looking with evil eyes.

They began pecking on the front window. Alex became frightened. All of a sudden, fog surrounded the air. His truck lights provided little help to see what was out in the fields. He began hearing footsteps on top of his truck.

"What's out there?" Alex asked himself.

It sounded like people were walking on top of his truck, trying to find a way in. Alex was too scared to leave his truck and find out what it was.

There were no cars out driving. Alex knew he would be stuck there for the night praying for his safety.

"The stories must have really been true. If I leave my truck, I will disappear into the darkness. To never be seen again. I won't take that chance." Alex thought to himself.

Alex turned his truck lights off and closed the curtains to his truck. He curled up in the back corner of his truck hoping morning would come soon. A few hours later, the noises stopped.

"Is it gone?" Alex asked himself.

What Alex wasn't told, if you stay hidden from the outside darkness, then it won't come near you. It wasn't until Alex turned everything off and went behind the curtains of his truck, that the darkness finally left him alone. He was lucky that night.

When daylight arose, Alex got his tire fixed and left the town of Doomsville, to never return again.

SCREAMING BRIDGE

While exploring the woods with his friends one day, Kevin heard screams echoing from a distance.

"Ahh!" Dorothy became startled.
"What was that?" Melody asked.
"Sounded like screams." Dorothy replied.

They all looked around. The children wanted to know where it was coming from.

"Where are they coming from?" Samuel asked.
"It's hard to tell. It echoes through the trees." Kevin replied.

Continuing to look around them,

"Maybe over there." Dorothy said.
"I think it's coming from this way." Terry said.

The children decided earlier in the day to explore through the woods and play in the creeks. It was starting to get late as sunset approached when the screaming began. They followed the screams until they ran into an old bridge in the middle of the woods.

"Look. It's the old bridge. The one talked about from the stories." Kevin said.
"Stories of an old road that use to run through here?" Terry asked.
"Yes. Where the little girl's body was found hanging from the bridge." Kevin replied.

"I wonder why she killed herself." Dorothy said.

They all stood looking at the bridge.

"I thought that was just a fake story." Melody said.
"Why would someone make up a story like that?" Dorothy asked.
"The girl hung herself after her parents died in a car crash." Samuel said.

Melody looked at Dorothy.

"I guess it is a real story." Melody said.
"What really happened?" Dorothy asked.

Everyone turned to Kevin. He was more knowledgeable than anyone else in the group.

"The dad lost control of the car and it went over the bridge. The daughter was sad and wanted to see her parents, so she hung herself from the same bridge." Kevin replied.

The children began to get a little scared. Parts of the bridge was crumbling off. They wasn't sure if they should get any closer to it. The old road was covered over with dirt and trees that had fallen on its' path. The road had been abandoned since the deaths. New roads were built shortly after. No one wanted to visit the bridge anymore. All of a sudden, screaming began again.

"Maybe it's the ghosts of the family." Melody said.
"The ghosts?" Dorothy asked.

They glanced at each other.

"Let's go check it out." Terry suggested.
"Can't you see the bridge is crumbling?" Dorothy asked.
"It doesn't seem that safe." Samuel said.

The children turned to the bridge.

"Just be careful." Kevin said as he started walking towards the bridge slowly.
"Come on. Let's follow close." Samuel said.
"Okay." Terry said as he followed.

They approached the bridge with caution. Suddenly, they heard a girl calling for help. Worried that someone was in trouble, the children began looking around, but couldn't find the girl. Wanting to explore further, but darkness had fallen.

"It's getting late." Samuel said.
"And it's dark." Dorothy said.
"We should be heading back home." Terry said.
"Wait. Who is that?" Kevin asked.

There had appeared to be a person under the bridge. It was a man wearing dirty clothes.

"It looks like a homeless man." Terry replied.
"Why would he be here?" Samuel asked.
"This is a scary place to live." Melody said.
"What is he doing?" Dorothy asked.

All five of them stared at the man.

"I think he is asleep." Melody replied.
"Or dead." Samuel said.
"He isn't moving." Terry said.

Once again, they looked at each other.

"He isn't dead. I can see him breathing." Kevin said.
"Go touch him." Terry suggested.
"Okay." Kevin said.

Kevin inched over quietly to the man. He made sure he was cautious around him.

"Hey mister. Are you okay?" Kevin asked.

The man didn't move.

"Mister." Kevin said a little louder.

The man suddenly sat up and tried to grab Kevin. He was frightened by the man's sudden movements.

"Ahhh!" The children yelled.
"Run!" Kevin shouted.

They all ran away from the bridge, back into the woods. The screams from the girl had disappeared more the further they ran.

"Is the man chasing us?" Dorothy asked.

"I don't think so." Terry replied.

Stopping to catch their breaths, they looked around them. They stayed close in fear that the man was near them.

"That man was going to get us." Melody said.
"He was scary looking." Terry claimed.

Continuing to catch their breaths,

"Listen, the screams stopped." Dorothy stated.
"Maybe the family doesn't like us." Melody said.

Terry looked confused. Everyone knew that the family couldn't be angry at them.

"We didn't do anything." Terry said.
"That's probably why no one goes near the bridge." Kevin claimed.
"The ghost family runs them off if they try." Samuel said.

Everyone could agree after the scare they had just experienced. No one wanted that experience again.

"I'm not going back there." Dorothy said.
"Me either." Melody said.

They all agreed they weren't going back. The children walked the rest of the way home together.

KILLER AMONG US

Renee and Caleb decided to go hiking one day. On the way to the woods, they ran into Mary and Reid.

"Where are you going?" Mary asked.
"We are going hiking." Renee replied.

Caleb looked over at Reid.

"Do you want to go?" Caleb asked.
"Yes." Reid replied.

The four of them trotted along towards the woods. A few minutes later they ran into Linda and Lincoln.

"Where are you all off to?" Linda asked.
"We are going hiking." Renee replied.

Lincoln glanced at Caleb.

"Sounds fun." Lincoln said.
"Come along." Caleb suggested.
"Okay." Linda said.

They began to walk away together. The children were off for a hike through the woods.

"Wait! I want to go too." Kristi hollered.
"Come on." Lincoln said.

Finally, the seven of them went into the woods and followed a hiking trail. After a few minutes, Lincoln noticed something was off about the group.

"Wasn't there seven of us?" Lincoln asked.

They all looked around.

"Mary is missing." Kristi said.
"Where did she go?" Renee asked.

The girls looked confused.

"I'm sure she turned around and went back. Let's keep going or we will not get out by dark." Reid said.

The group of six continued along the path. They came upon a small waterfall.

"We can rest here for a few." Lincoln said.
"Yes I'm tired." Renee said.

The girls sat on a big rock. They stretched a little and then noticed something.

"Where is Caleb?" Kristi asked.

They all looked around again.

"Maybe he turned around too." Linda replied.

No one knew what to say.

"Okay this is getting weird." Kristi said.
"Everyone stay close. We should keep moving. This path takes us in a circle back around to the beginning. We should be back before dark if we stay on track." Reid explained.

The five of them continued onto the trail. Awhile later, they came to a small bridge that crossed over a creek. They stopped to glance at a map.

"We should be back to the car soon according to the map." Reid said.
"Where is Linda?" Kristi asked.

Everyone looked around. No one could figure out why they were disappearing.

"Why is it that everyone is disappearing?" Reid asked.

Scared, they all looked confused. The remaining children began to fear that they were next.

"I don't like this." Renee said.
"Someone is killing us off." Kristi said.

Reid looked at Kristi.

"No one is killing us." Reid said.
"You don't know about these woods." Renee said.

No one knew what was going on.

"My brother told me a story once." Kristi said.
"What story is that?" Reid asked.

Everyone listened to Kristi.

"A group of kids went hiking a long time ago. They disappeared into the woods and was never heard from again. No one ever solved the mystery of the missing kids." Kristi explained.

Reid was confused.

"If you knew this, Why did you come with us?" Reid asked.
"I forgot about the story until now. He told me last year about it." Kristi replied.

Everyone stopped to think for a few moments. Reid wasn't sure to believe Kristi.

"Maybe you and your brother are playing tricks on us. You are telling the story." Reid said.
"I'm not! This is real. We need to get out of here." Kristi said.

Renee grew annoyed.

"No reason to argue. We need to stay more alert." Renee said.
"Let's just get out of here." Reid said.

As they began to cross the bridge,

"Lincoln is gone." Kristi said.
"What?" Reid asked in confusion.

The three looked at each other.

"See, you two were so busy arguing that another one of us disappeared." Renee said.

Kristi pointed to Reid.

"It's his fault." Kristi said.

Reid looked confused towards Kristi. He didn't know why Kristi would blame him.

"I'm not making anyone disappear." Reid said.
"I'm not either." Kristi said.

Once again, Renee was annoyed by the two. They had argued too much at this point.

"Stop! Let's get out of these woods now." Renee said.

They continued along the path once more. Coming to the end,

"I hear something coming." Kristi said.

The three ran out of the woods. There sat all of their friends.

"What happened to you all?" Reid asked.
"We don't know." Caleb replied.

"One minute we were walking, the next we were sitting here." Lincoln explained.

"We figured you would join us sooner or later." Linda said.

Reid was extremely confused at this point.

"Let's go home." Reid said.

All seven children returned home safely and swore to avoid the woods from now on.

Island Scares

"A beautiful island sat right off the east coast. Many would visit daily. A ferry took everyone from the states to the island. There was no road that led to the island itself. It was full of big colorful trees. Anyone's dream to live. One day, a rich couple came along and bought the island. They stopped all visitors from coming.

A mansion was built at the top of a small hill where the couple could look out and see the states. It was like a dream come true for the woman. Only one thing was missing. Children. She had it planned to fill the island with lots of children of her own. Many that they could share their fortune with. Destiny had something else in mind.

Every time the woman got pregnant, she miscarried. The doctors told her to give up trying. Eventually, the woman died sad and lonely. After her death, the woman's ghost walked the island at night in search for children. Visitors began coming to the island again and camping. There have been many reports over the centuries of this woman ghost trying to steal children."

The present day,

"Who believes these stories?" Rose asked.
"They are true." A boy said.
"You will see when we get to the island." Another boy said.

Rose and Lilly met up with their cousins Autumn, Bella, and Candice on the ferry. Their family decided to camp on the most popular island. On the journey over, they joined in on a group of story tellers. The girls didn't seem to believe what was being said. Once to the island,

"Wow. Look at it Lilly." Rose said.
"I see." Lilly said.

They both stood looking over the island. They seen the beautiful trees and the mansion on top of the small hill. The island was full of people visiting. They would be staying at the camping area below the mansion.

"Mommy, can we visit the mansion?"
"Of course we can."

The ladies took their girls to visit the mansion. They were allowed to explore freely if they stayed close. The girls went from room to room to look around.

"These are big bedrooms." Lilly said.
"They were built for the couple's children that they never had." Autumn said.

Lilly laughed.

"Did you believe that story?" Lilly asked.
"I did my research before coming." Autumn replied.

Rose became curious.

"So it's true?" Rose asked.
"Yes, it's all true." Candice said.
"At night, you will see the lady's ghost." Bella claimed.

Rose shrugged the girls away.

"I don't believe it." Rose said.

"She will come when you are sleeping. You may or may not be here in the morning." Autumn said.

Rose was in disbelief.

"If you say so." Rose said as she walked away.

After exploring, they all went to eat and explore the rest of the island. They also swam on a small beach area of the island. While playing in the sand, Rose overheard other children talking about the ghost woman. She decided to listen.

"How come this is the first I'm hearing about these stories?" Rose asked.

"You are still young. I heard of them and then told my sisters." Autumn said.

"Well. I don't know if these are really true." Rose said.

"Don't believe it if you don't want to." Autumn said.

"I believe it." Lilly said.

Rose decided to go play elsewhere. After a while, they went back to camp. The sun was going down and the moon coming up. The girls decided to go to bed for the night.

"Hope to see you in the morning." Autumn said.

Rose said her goodnight and went to bed. She couldn't sleep much with thought of the story about the woman. She felt sad that life had denied the woman of children. Eventually, Rose became tired and began to drift off into sleep. Suddenly, she heard noises outside her tent.

"What was that?" Rose questioned herself.

Rose began to glance around inside her tent. She seen a shadow figure of a woman walking around. She was frightened by the thoughts of the story being true.

"Maybe the story was true, and now the woman is coming to get me." Rose thought to herself.

The noises of footsteps were faint. Rose grew scared to sleep. She had though the ghost was waiting on her to fall asleep.

"If I stay up all night, the woman can't come for me while I'm sleeping." Rose continued to think.

Staying up until sunrise, Rose was exhausted. She heard her family awake when she finally dozed off to sleep. She knew she was safe at that point. Her mother checked on her.

"She must be really tired this morning." Mother said.
"I will wake her." Lilly said.
"No, let her sleep. We will have breakfast and then check on her again." Mother said as she walked away.
"I hope she's not sick." Aunt said.
"I'm sure she is fine." Mother said.

They all had breakfast and got dressed for the day. All of a sudden, Rose let out a scream. Everyone went running to her.

"Get her off me!" Rose screamed.
"Who?" Mother asked.

"Get her off me!" Rose screamed again.
"No one is on you." Mother said.
"Wake up Rose!" Lilly hollered at Rose.

Rose finally arose. Heart racing, trying to catch her breath.

"You were having a nightmare Rose." Mother stated.

She looked around at everyone staring at her. Rose became a little embarrassed.

"It was the woman wasn't it?" Autumn asked.
"What woman?" Mother asked.
"The woman that hunts for children on the island." Bella replied.
"That's an old story and isn't true." Mother said.
"It is true Mom. I seen her shadow last night outside my tent. I thought she had come for me, so I stayed awake all night." Rose claimed.
"That is why you were so tired this morning." Candice said.
"I seen the shadow too." Lilly said.
"Don't be scared Rose. That was me last night. I got up to check on everyone." Aunt said.

Everyone looked at each other. After a few moments, Rose got up and ate. She then got dressed and joined her family for a day out before heading back home on the ferry. Rose didn't speak of her island experience ever again.

SCARECROW'S FIELD

Jason and his friends decided to spend the day at the orchard together. Their parents dropped them off for a few hours. The boys played big games that the orchard had set out in random sections of the yard. They also fed the animals and took a hayride. While on the hayride with his friends, Jason overheard conversations from other children.

"Let's check out the scarecrow field." A boy said.
"You know we are not allowed there." Another boy said.

His friends joined the conversation.

"What's the scarecrow field?" Charles asked.
"It's the field on the other side of the corn. The scarecrow was put there as a grave marking." One boy replied.

The boys looked at each other in curiosity. They were into scary things to a point.

"Grave?" Bradley asked.
"A long time ago, a man dug a deep hole in the ground. When kids came through the field, he threw them into the hole." The boy replied.
"The children died in there before anyone found them." Another boy said.
"I'm telling this story." The first boy said.

They all gathered closer to listen.

"At night you can hear their screams for help if you are near the field. The town filled the hole in with dirt and left the children together. The people put the scarecrow there to keep other children away from the field." The boy continued.

The hayride ended and they all got off.

"Do you believe them?" Jeremy asked.
"No. Let's go to the maze now." Jason replied.

The boys went into the corn maze. They took a couple wrong turns and got lost.

"It's this way." Charles said.
"We already went that way." Jason said.
"I think it's over here." Bradley said.
"No, the exit is this way. I can see an opening through there." Jeremy said.
"Come on. Let's check it out." Jason said.

The four boys made there way through the corn towards the opening. Once they made it out, the boys couldn't believe what they were seeing. It was a big field.

"This is the field the others were talking about." Charles said.
"Look, there's the scarecrow." Bradley said.

They looked across the field.

"That must be where all the kids are in a grave together." Jason said.

The boys came out of the wrong side of the corn. They stood gazing around at everything. The field was scary to them. The scarecrow looked old with strings of dried hay falling out of it. Big black birds landed on the scarecrow's arms picking him apart slowly.

"I'm going into the field to check it out." Jason said.
"You heard we are not suppose to be in the field." Jeremy said.
"No one is here." Charles said.

Jeremy was scared, but followed the other boys in. They wanted to observe the scarecrow more. As the boys approached it, small gusts of wind began to blow. A few of the boys grew frightened. They wasn't sure if the scarecrow would get them for being in his field.

"We should leave." Charles said.
"Don't be scared of a scarecrow." Jason said.
"There are bodies under it in a grave." Jeremy said.
"If the story is true." Bradley said.
"Stay close." Jason said.

Continuing towards the scarecrow, Jeremy was hesitant. The scarecrow began to shake. Big black crows flew in circles around them. Dark clouds formed in the sky.

"I don't like this." Charles said.
"I'm scared." Jeremy said.

At this point, the boys were standing in front of the scarecrow, on top of the said grave. Jason reached out to touch the scarecrow.

"Don't touch it." Jeremy said.

It was too late. Jason had touched the scarecrow. It instantly shook harder. Its eyes glowed brightly. The sky became dark over the scarecrow. Black birds began to crow loudly as they started to attack the boys.

"RUN!" Jason screamed.

They screamed and ran out of the field, back through the corn. The boys didn't stop running until they came to an older couple. They were frightened by what had just happened.

"Slow down. What is going on?" The man asked.

The boys were in a frantic.

"The scarecrow!" The boys yelled.

They ran behind the man to hide. The boys were afraid the scarecrow would come after them.

"You boys shouldn't be in that field." The man said.
"It's going to get us!" Jeremy hollered.

The man turned around to face the boys.

"Nothing is going to get you. Calm down." The man said.
"Where are your parents?" The woman asked.
"They dropped us off here." Charles replied.

The couple began to walk away.

"Come on. I'll show you boys the way out." The man said.

The four boys followed the man. Eventually, they found the correct way out of the corn. As they sat to wait on their parents to pick them up, they drank apple cider.

"These are really good." Bradley said.
"I know." Charles said.

They sat enjoying their drinks together.

"I don't ever want to go back to that field." Jeremy said.

The boys looked at each other. They honestly had no intentions on going back.

"We are never going back." Jason said.
"I thought the crows were going to eat us alive." Charles said.
"Me too." Jeremy said.
"I'm glad we ran out of there when we did." Bradley said.

Continuing with their Apple cider,

"Let's not tell our parents." Jason said.
"Why not?" Charles asked.
"They may never let us meet up again." Jason replied.
"Okay." Charles said.

The boys swore to never tell anyone what happened. They would never visit the scarecrow field again.

BAD DREAMS

Alicia kept having the same falling nightmare every night. As much as she tried, Alicia couldn't get it off her mind. One night, another nightmare came. Mom rushed in to check on Alicia.

"Are you okay?" Mom asked.

Catching her breath, Alicia sat up in bed.

"I'm okay." Alicia replied.

Alicia explained the dream to Mom, who assured her it was just a dream. After awhile of sitting with her daughter, Mom went back to bed. The next day, Alicia went out to play with her friends. Wandering about, they ran into an old water tower. Everyone decided to climb up the stairs of the tower. As Alicia began to step up on the ladder, she remembered her dream.

"Are you going to come?" Brenda asked.

Alicia turned to her friends.

"I can't climb up there." Alicia replied.
"Why?" Katy asked.

Being hesitant to tell her friends about the dream,

"I just can't. You go on without me." Alicia replied.
"It's not scary." Danny said.

She glanced up the tower.

"I'm not scared." Alicia said.
"Then why won't you come?" Luke asked.

Giving in, Alicia finally told her friends about the dream.

"I had a dream that I fell off of something high. I don't want to take a chance." Alicia explained.
"Okay." Brenda said.

Alicia stood back and watched her friends climb and have fun. She knew she was safer on the ground. Her dream was a warning to her. When the dream came back to her, she knew she couldn't climb the tower.

After that day, the dream stopped. Everything seemed to go back to normal in Alicia's life. With no more dreams, it was great.

"My dreams stopped." Alicia said.
"See, I told you everything would be fine." Mom said.

One night a few months later, Alicia had another bad dream. This time, she was drowning instead of falling. She couldn't tell where she was at, but she felt a current pulling her under the water. The dream repeated on several occasions.

"Mom, the dreams are back." Alicia said.

Mom looked at her daughter.

"You are not going to fall off anything." Mom said.

"No, this time I am drowning." Alicia explained.

Mom seemed confused.

"These are just dreams." Mom said.

Alicia grabbed Mom.

"I think my dreams are warning me." Alicia said.
"You will be fine. Go out and play." Mom said as she walked away.

A few days later, Mom surprised the kids with a beach trip. Everyone was excited once they arrived. Not Alicia. She had a bad feeling come upon her. Caution set in once she walked towards the water.

"Go ahead, get in." Mom said.

Mom nudged Alicia towards the water.

"No thank you." Alicia responded.

Confused, Mom began to question.

"Why not?" Mom asked.

Alicia turned towards her mom.

"The dreams are warning me." Alicia replied.
"You can't walk around scared because you had a dream." Mom said.

She thought for a few moments.

"I will sit by the bank and put my feet in." Alicia said as she walked down the beach.

Again, after that day the dreams stopped. Alicia knew the dreams were warnings, but wasn't sure why the dreams had come on all of a sudden. Deciding to go to her Grandpa, she wanted answers.

"Grandpa, I keep having these dreams." Alicia said.

Grandpa looked at Alicia.

"What kind of dreams?" Grandpa asked.
"I had a dream of falling off something. Then when I came to a tower, I refused to climb it and the dreams stopped. A few months later I had a dream of drowning. Then when I refused to swim at the beach, the dreams stopped." Alicia explained.

Grandpa looked confused.

"How long have you been having these dreams?" Grandpa asked.
"They started last year." Alicia replied.
"That's about the time your grandma passed." Grandpa said.

Alicia thought for a moment.

"Yes, you are right." Alicia said.
"The gift was passed to you." Grandpa said.
"Gift?" Alicia asked.
"Your grandma had a gift. She had prediction warning dreams."

Grandpa explained.

"I knew that's what they were." Alicia said to herself.

"Does your Mom know?" Grandpa asked.

She looked at Grandpa shaking her head yes.

"She didn't inherit the gift. It is only passed down after the person who has the gift dies. It went to you." Grandpa explained.

"How come Mom didn't inherit it?" Alicia asked.

"It tends to go to the youngest. That would be you." Grandpa said.

Alicia sat with Grandpa talking awhile. Then he left. She began with another dream shortly after. This time it was a car crash on a bridge. Alicia told Mom, but she didn't believe her.

"Get in the car. We have to go." Mom said.

"I had a dream we were in an accident." Alicia said.

Mom thought Alicia was being defiant, so she put her in the car. Alicia was scared the whole time in the car. They approached a bridge. Just as Alicia began to say something, another car crashed into the side of their car and almost flipped them over a bridge.

"I told you." Alicia said.

Mom looked at Alicia.

"You inherited Grandma's gift." Mom said.

"I know. I talked to Grandpa." Alicia responded.

From that day forward, Mom took caution to what Alicia dreamed.

RUSTIC CABOOSE

While out with friends one day, Derek ran into an old abandoned train caboose.

"Look over there." Derek said.

Everyone glanced over through the woods.

"Wow!" Joshua said.
"Let's go check it out." Cameron said.

The boys went over to check out the caboose. As they stood at the steps, the boys began to hear knocking.

"What was that?" Cameron asked.

They looked around them.

"Sounded like knocking." Derek replied.
"Someone must be in there." Joshua said.

Cameron glanced over at the caboose.

"Go check it out." Cameron suggested.
"You check it out." Derek responded.

They argued with each other about who would go check it out. After a few moments,

"Knock, knock, knock." Came from the caboose.

The three became scared.

"There it is again." Joshua said.
"Who's in there?" Derek asked loudly.

There was no response.

"I'm going to go see." Derek said.
"Be careful." Cameron said.

Derek slowly climbed the steps and approached the door. He knocked twice. No response. He knocked two more times. Then suddenly,

"Knock, knock!" Again came from the inside of the caboose.

Derek reached for the door.

"Don't open it." Joshua said.
"Be quiet. I want to see who is in there." Derek responded.

Suddenly, Derek heard someone walking around inside. He paused. He wasn't sure if he should open the door at that point. Then, it was silent.

Derek began to climb on top of the train.

"What are you doing?" Cameron asked.
"I'm checking out the top." Derek replied.

Joshua decided to be brave.

"I'll go with you." Joshua said.
"You guys are crazy." Cameron said.

Derek and Joshua climbed on top of the caboose. After a few moments of walking around,

"Bang! Bang! Bang!" Came from the inside of the caboose.

Loud banging on the walls began. Derek and Joshua became so scared they climbed off the Caboose quickly. Once everything calmed down, they approached the train again.

"You are going to get on again?" Cameron asked.
"I want to know who is in there." Derek replied.

Derek banged on the door. There was no answer. He swung the door open and stood staring into the darkness. It was quiet and dark. He couldn't see anything.

"You should get away from there." Cameron whispered out.

Cameron and Joshua stood back away from the caboose in fear. Suddenly, a dark figure lunged out of the darkness. It had red glowing eyes and growled at Derek. He became frightened and screamed.

"Get out of here!" Derek screamed.
"What is it?" Joshua asked.

They turned towards the caboose to see the dark shadow.

"Run!" Cameron yelled.

The three boys ran as fast as they could out of the woods. As they got to the street, they seen the old man of the town sitting out on his front porch. They ran to him.

"What are you running from boys?" The old man asked.
"The shadow figure from the caboose!" Joshua Hollered.

Cameron covered his eyes.

"Is it gone?" Cameron asked.
"Yes." Derek said.
"You guys met the ghost conductor." The man calmly said.

They looked at the old man.

"The what?" Joshua asked.
"Ghost driver of the train." The old man replied.

The boys were confused.

"The train derailed from the tracks a long time ago when I was a kid. It threw the driver out the door and he was crushed by his own train." The old man explained.

Derek, Cameron, and Joshua stared at each other.

"They eventually hauled the train away, but left the caboose. It's said that the ghost of the driver lives there. He wasn't a pleasant man." The old man continued.

Cameron became curious.

"What do you mean?" Cameron asked.
"He hated children." The old man replied.
"Why?" Joshua asked.
"No one knew. He was mean to any child who came around him." The old man replied.

The boys didn't like hearing this.

"You boys should go home and stay away from there." The old man warned.

They decided to listen to the man. The boys went home to never return to the caboose again.

RED BARN

Doors kept slamming loudly. It was dark and scary. Harry couldn't sleep with all the noise.

"Are you awake?" Harry asked.
"Yes." Harold replied.
"The wind must be strong." Harry said.
"I hear all the noise." Harold responded.

Harry and his brother tried to sleep again. The noise annoyed Harold. It was too loud for him.

"I'm going out there to fix those doors. I need some sleep tonight." Harold said.

Harold began getting out of bed.

"It's scary out there at night." Harry said.
"Nothing to be scared of." Harold responded.

Harry didn't want his brother to go. He tried to talk him out of going. Nothing seemed to work.

"It's not our barn and it sits out near the woods. You can't go out there." Harry said.
"I can't sleep with all the noise." Harold said.

The brothers decided to go out to the barn and shut the doors so they could sleep. The wind was strong and the air foggy. Harry found this scary as he made his way with his brother to the barn.

"I'm glad I brought this lantern." Harry said.
"It helps very little with all the fog." Harold responded.
"But at least it's not completely dark." Harry said.

As the boys got closer to the barn, they began to hear voices. Harry didn't like this.

"Someone is out here." Harry said.
"It might be the neighbor going to the barn too. Let's go see." Harold said.

Harry grew scared.

"Maybe we should go back to the house." Harry suggested.
"Let's make sure." Harold said.

The boys approached the barn. It was old, red in color. Hay was laying around.

"I hear the horses." Harry said.
"Let's go in." Harold said.

Once inside, there was silence. The boys looked around them. Horses were in stalls moving around. The barn was big and had hay thrown everywhere.

"It's a mess in here." Harry said.
"The hay is probably thrown out for the horses to eat on during the day." Harold responded.

The windows of the barn had dirt covering them. There was a ladder leading to a loft area on the other side of the barn. The lantern shined through the barn. After a few moments, they began hearing light cries. This stirred the horses up a little.

"Do you hear that?" Harry asked.
"It sounds like someone crying." Harold replied.

Hey glanced around them.

"Where's it coming from?" Harry asked.
"I think the loft area." Harold replied.

Harry followed his brother over to the ladder. As they looked up,

"Did you see that?" Harry asked.
"Yes." Harold replied.

The boys continued to stare up towards the loft.

"It was a shadow." Harry said.
"Someone is up there." Harold said.

Harold was determined to find out who was in the barn. Being scared, Harry stayed at the bottom of the stairs while his brother climbed into the loft.

"Do you see anything?" Harry asked.

About that time, Harold slipped down the ladder screaming. This frightened Harry.

"Get out of here now!" Harold yelled.

Both boys ran out of the barn quickly.

"What was it?" Harry asked.
"A girl ghost came at me." Harold replied.

Harry stood frightened looking around him.

"Let's go." Harold said.

The boys ran back towards their house. On the way, they seen their neighbor.

"What were you doing in my barn?" The neighbor asked.
"The doors were slamming and keeping us awake." Harry replied.
"We couldn't sleep with all the noise." Harold said.

The neighbor stared at the two boys.

"There is something in there." Harry said.
"We seen a shadow figure and heard cries." Harold said.

Continuing to stare at the boys in silence, the neighbor found their story amusing.

"My brother went to the loft." Harry said.
"I seen a girl ghost." Harold said.

The boys rambled on about what happened.

"You haven't heard the story?" The neighbor asked.

Harry and Harold looked at the neighbor.

"What story?" Harold asked.
"A couple use to own this home a long time ago. They had a little girl. One day, their daughter was playing too close to the horses. The horse kicked her so hard it killed her. That was their only child." The neighbor explained.

They stared at the neighbor not knowing what to say about his story. This made them sad.

"I hear the ghost of the girl crying every night since I moved in. I never thought anyone else would hear her." The neighbor continued.

Suddenly, the cries began again. The boys got scared and told the neighbor they had to get home. Harry and Harold never went back onto the neighbor's property. They stayed away from the haunted big red barn.

GREEN WITCHES

While staying with grandma for a weekend, Luna and Levi had quite a spooky adventure. They were out playing with friends when they discovered an old worn down house in the back woods of a park. It was small with cracked windows and falling apart.

"Look at this little house." Levi said.

Everyone looked at the house.

"It's old." Ethan said.
"No one could live in that." Mickey said.
"Let's go check it out." Levi said.

Luna was unsure.

"We can't trespass on that property." Luna said.
"It's a tiny house in the middle of the woods." Avery said.

After a few moments, the children decided to sneak up to the windows. They wanted to know what was inside. As they peaked in the windows, the children saw something unbelievable.

"Who are they?" Ethan asked.
"I don't know, but what are they doing?" Levi responded and asked.

Two women were in there. One looking in an old book. The other stirring something in a huge pot. Black cats were scattered everywhere.

The children didn't have a good feeling about this.

"Are they doing a spell?" Avery asked.
"That's what it looks like." Luna replied.

Suddenly the women turned to the side. The children were able to get a better look at them.

"They are green." Luna said.
"They are ugly." Mickey said.

They continued to observe the women.

"They are scary looking." Avery said.
"We should leave." Mickey said.

About that time, Luna slipped and bumped the window ledge. This made the women look at them. The children became scared and jumped away from the window.

"They saw us." Levi said.
"What are we going to do?" Ethan asked.

The green women slammed the door open and seen the children standing in the front of their house.

"They are going to get us." Avery said.

The women began yelling and walking towards the children. They became frightened and ran away from the house.

"Let's go!" Levi yelled.

Almost reaching home, the children saw a few older kids out playing ball. They approached them with their story.

"You are never going to believe what we saw." Luna said.
"What did you see?" One boy asked.
"Green women." Mickey replied.

The older boys stared at the children.

"It's true." Avery said.
"Two of them." Ethan said.

The older boys weren't responding much.

"Don't you believe us?" Levi asked.
"We had the same thing happen to us at your age." Another boy replied.

The children were confused.

"What do you mean?" Ethan asked.
"The witches." The third boy said.

Ethan looked at his friends.

"Witches?" Luna asked.
"They did look like witches." Avery responded.

The older boys began to explain.

"The witches were hung years before we were born." The first boy said.

"Why?" Levi asked.

"For setting spells on the town's children." The second boy said.

The children became scared as the older boys continued with their story about the witches.

"Their ghosts have been known to come back on full moons to create more spells." The third boy explained.

"Yeah, but they have been unsuccessful." The first boy said.

Mickey was confused.

"They were ghosts?" Mickey asked.

"Yes, ghosts can come in full body." The second boy replied.

As the children looked at each other,

"They seemed so real." Mickey said to his friends.

"Only if they can catch a child, then they can create a spell that will work." The third boy explained.

They looked back to the older boys.

"Never go near that house on a full moon." The first boy said.

"They come after children." The second boy said.

Being frightened,

"We will never go near that house again." Levi said.

"No, never." Luna said.
"We promise." Ethan said.

The older three were happy with the children's responses.

"Good." The first boy said.
"Now go home. It's getting dark." The second boy said.

They began to walk away.

"And stay home!" The third boy hollered.

The children swore to never go back. They went home and kept the secret about the green witches.

"I never seen them go into the woods." The first boy said.
"We need to keep a better eye out." The second boy said.
"Yes, you know what could happen if them witches ever get a hold of a child." The third boy said.
"We can't let that happen." The second boy said.

The older boys continued playing ball until all the children were inside. They made sure no one went towards the woods, keeping their town safe.

CRUISE SHIP

Beth and Randy were on a cruise with their family when they encountered something from beyond for the first time. The ship had separate sleeping quarters for each family. It also had eating areas and activities for everyone aboard.

After a day full of activities and eating, Beth and Randy were tired. They returned back to their sleeping quarters with their family. Mom tucked them into bed and they said their goodnight. In the middle of the night, Beth was awakened by a knock on the door.

"Knock, knock." From the door.
"Who is that?" Beth asked herself.

Beth glanced around her. Everyone was sleeping. She decided to wake her brother up.

"Someone is knocking at the door. You need to get out of bed and look." Beth said.

Randy opened the door. Looking down the halls, he noticed a little boy rolling a ball around. His parents were not in sight. Beth and Randy walked towards the boy.

"Where are your parents?" Randy asked.
"Hey, stop." Beth said to the boy.
"Come on." Randy said as he grabbed his sister's hand.

The little boy took off running with his ball. Randy and Beth followed him down the hallway. He seemed to move quickly as they tried to keep up with him.

"Where are you going?" Beth asked as the boy continued running.

Beth was confused.

"Maybe he is lost." Beth said.

Randy thought for a moment.

"He probably needs help finding his room. We can find his parents." Randy said.
"Let's just keep following him." Beth said.

The two continued to follow the little boy through the hallways. He kept disappearing on them.

"Where did he go now?" Beth asked.
"I think this way." Randy replied.

All of a sudden, Randy and Beth ran into two other children venturing the hallways also.

"What are you doing up?" The kids asked.
"We are chasing the little boy." Beth replied.

The other two children stared at Beth and Randy. They were all in confusion.

"We are too." The kids said.
"Did he wake you up?" Beth asked.

The two other children looked at each other. It had seemed like they all had the same experience.

"Yes." The kids replied.
"Do you know where he went?" Randy asked.

The children began hearing laughing.

"He is this way." The kids said.

They went running down the steps. With caution, the children followed the laughing into a broiler room. It was dark, hot, and scary. Steam was coming out of the broiler.

"Are you sure he is in here?" Beth asked.

They glanced around them.

"This is where the laughing stopped. He must be in here somewhere." Randy replied.

The door suddenly slammed open. The children turned around quickly to look.

"What are you doing in here?" A man asked.

The children looked scared.

"We followed a little boy." Randy said.

The man looked at them strangely.

"You are not supposed to be in here." The man said.

"The boy woke us up and we followed him down here. We thought he was lost." Beth explained.

The man kindly interrupted.

"That same little boy once explored his way in here too a long time ago." The man said.

Beth was confused.

"What do you mean?" Beth asked.

He looked at Beth.

"He wandered away from his parents one day and got too close to the broilers." The man explained.

They listened to the man in curiosity. The children were intrigued by the story.

"One of the workers tried to reach him, but it was too late. He fell into the broiler and burned." The man continued.

Beth and Randy were shocked of what the man was saying. The other two children stood silently.

"His ghost tries to lead other children who come on the ship to this room." The man said.

The children grew frightened by the man's story. They had been following a ghost.

"You need to go back to your rooms now. You shouldn't be wandering these halls." The man said firmly.

Everyone began walking away.

"And stay there before you get hurt too. Don't be out following ghosts." The man continued.

Once back upstairs, they parted ways back to their rooms. No one wandered the hall the rest of the night. The next day, they left the ship with their parents to travel back home. Randy and Beth never spoke about their ghost adventure to anyone.

UNDERGROUND TRACKS

Playing with friends out in the fields, Albert discovered hidden steps behind a bunch of broken tree branches piled on the ground. It led underground somewhere.

"I found some type of stairs." Albert said.

Everyone went over to check the stairs out. They found them quite interesting.

"Where do they lead?" Summer asked.
"Let's find out." Conner responded.

Jamie was hesitant.

"We shouldn't go down there." Jamie said.
"No one will know." Conner said.

As they began down the steps slowly,

"It looks dark." Summer said.
"I have a pocket flashlight." Albert said.

They all checked their pockets.

"I have a light on my phone too." Jamie said.

The children continued to the bottom of the steps. It was chilly and dark. They could see only by the brightness of their lights. This was enough to see a few feet in front of them.

"I think it's an old underground railroad station." Albert said.
"It's dirty and scary down here." Summer said.

They continued to observe their surroundings.

"Let's go check out those tracks." Conner said.

Everyone ran over to the tracks together.

"I wonder where they lead." Jamie said.
"Let's follow them." Albert suggested.

The children walked down the tracks. After a few moments, they came upon an old train cart.

"I think workers used these a long time ago. I remember seeing these in my history books." Conner said.
"Let's ride in it." Albert said.
"I don't think we should." Summer said.
"Nothing bad will happen. It's just an old train box." Albert said.

They got on the little train cart and slowly began down the tracks observing along the way.

"This isn't that bad." Jamie said.
"It's kind of fun." Summer said.

Suddenly, the cart got faster.

"What's happening?" Summer asked.
"The train picked up on speed." Conner replied.

Summer became concerned.

"I'm scared." Summer said.
"It will be okay." Jamie said.
"It's getting faster again." Summer said.
"Hold on tight." Albert said.

The children hovered tightly.

"Where's it going to take us?" Summer asked.
"I don't know." Jamie replied.
"We have to stop at some point." Conner said.

Looking forward,

"Is that a dead end ahead of us?" Albert asked.
"We are going to crash!" Jamie shouted.

Still tightly hanging on,

"Hang on everyone!" Albert hollered.

All of a sudden, the train cart hit a dead end and tipped sideways throwing the children out of the box. It took them a few minutes to calm down.

"Where are we?" Jamie asked.

Observing around them, they appeared to be in a room full of dirt. It was smelly and dusty. White bone structures mixed in the dirt covered the floor of the room.

"What are these?" Summer asked.

They all bent to look.

"Bones." Conner replied.
"Human?" Jamie asked.

Albert took a closer look.

"Looks more like animal bones." Albert replied.
"How can you be sure?" Summer asked.
"Human bones are bigger." Albert replied.

Looking around more, Albert noticed a bigger bone. He pulled it out of the dirt.

"Now this is a human skull." Albert said.

Everyone came to look. The skull looked cracked.

"What happened to the person?" Summer asked.
"Maybe he was killed." Conner replied.

They began hearing whispering and footsteps around them. The children were scared.

"Let's get out of here." Jamie said.

The children made their way out of the underground railroad. As they reached the outside, a groundskeeper approached them.

"What are u doing down there?" The groundskeeper asked.
"We were just looking around." Albert replied.
"I use to work the underground. It was an old railroad station." The groundskeeper said.

They stared at him to listen.

"What happened to it?" Jamie asked.
"There was an explosion one day that killed several men and injured others. I'm one of the survivors. I try to keep this place hidden." The groundskeeper explained.

The four glanced at each other.

"We heard whispers and footsteps." Conner said.
"Ghosts of those who were killed, roam around down there and they are not friendly with visitors." The groundskeeper continued.

The children became frightened. They turned to go home.

"And don't tell anyone about this place or the ghosts will come to haunt you." The groundskeeper said as the children walked away.

Albert, Conner, Jamie, and Summer went home and never talked about their underground adventure. They never returned to the place again.

SEWER ADVENTURES

Playing kickball with her friends was Annie's favorite thing to do. The girls were in competition to keep up with the boys around the neighborhood. Daphne kicked the ball too hard and it rolled into an open sewer hole. The other girls didn't like this.

"Now we don't have a ball." Amber said.

The girls looked at Daphne.

"I didn't mean to kick it down there. It was an accident. I kicked the ball too hard." Daphne said.
"We could go get it." Annie said.
"I'm not going down there." Dakota said.

They thought for a moment.

"We will climb down, grab the ball, and come back up. It will be quick." Annie said.
"Alright, but we need to hurry before someone sees us. I don't want to be in trouble." Amber said.

The girls climbed down the ladder slowly that led into the sewer. After reaching the bottom, they looked around.

"How do people work down here?" Dakota asked.
"It's full of water." Daphne said.
"My feet are so wet." Amber said.

They were standing in knee high waters. It was cold and the air moist. They wanted to get out of there quick.

"Let's just find the ball and leave." Dakota said.

Glancing around,

"I don't see it." Amber said.
"It couldn't have gone far." Daphne said.

Continuing to look,

"Let's walk down this way and look." Annie said.
"You want me to walk through this?" Amber asked.
"We are already wet. It won't hurt you." Daphne replied.

Staying close to each other, the girls began walking through the sewers of town searching for their ball.

"We will never find it in these waters."
"I think we are lost."

Evidently, they took too many turns to remember how to get back. Now they were searching for a way out. All of a sudden, the girls began seeing dark shadows on the walls.

"Did you see that?" Amber asked.

The four were frightened.

"We need to get out of here." Amber said.

"What were those shadows from?" Dakota asked.
"Maybe the killer clown is down here. I watched them movies." Amber replied.

They looked at each other.

"That's not real." Daphne said.
"Yes, it is. He eats kids." Amber said.

As they continued walking through the waters, splashing began behind them.

"It's behind us!" Amber shouted.

The girls took off running while grabbing at each other's shirts. They were scared as they ran away.

"Hurry, go!" Dakota hollered.
"Move out of my way!" Annie screamed.

They eventually came to an opening. The four were freaking out on each other thinking a killer clown was going to get them. Daphne had enough of the arguing.

"Stop! We need to calm down and find a way out together." Daphne said.
"Look! I see light." Annie said.

The girls slowly made their way over towards the light in hopes of a way out.

"It's a way out." Dakota said.

The four climbed up the ladder out of the sewer. They were happy to finally be out of there. The girls ended up on the other side of town. This was far from where they started.

"How did we get this far?" Amber asked.
"We must of really took some wrong turns. I didn't realize we went that far." Annie responded.
"Let's go home." Daphne said.

On the way back, they ran into the boys.

"Why are you so wet?" Brandon asked.
"We were playing kickball and it went into the sewers." Annie replied.
"We tried to find it, but it's gone." Dakota said.

The boys stared at the girls.

"You went into the sewers?" Kyle asked.
"Haven't you heard about the little girl?" Brandon asked.

The girls were confused.

"What little girl?" Annie asked.

The boys began to tell the legend of the girl while the girls listened closely.

"The town was flooded a long time ago. A little girl got sucked down into the sewers and drowned. It was a horrible sight to see according to many of the town's people." Brandon said.

This scared the girls as the boys continued.

"Her body was never found. They searched for weeks with no luck." Kyle said.
"Her ghost roams the sewers through town. Sometimes you can hear her splashing down there." Brandon said.

It was silent for a few moments. The girls had remembered how there was splashing behind them in the sewers. Also, the shadows on the walls. They thought the story must be true.

"She probably took your ball to have something to play with at night." Kyle said.

The four girls looked at each other.

"She can have the ball." Annie said.
"I'm not going back down there." Dakota said.
"Me either." Daphne said.
"Let's go home and change." Amber said.

They all agreed the little girl could keep the ball. Being too scared to take it back, the girls weren't going to cry over losing it. They returned home to change and get another. Then, they continued to play outside staying away from the sewers this time.

BEHIND THE WATERFALL

The lake was big and deep enough to swim in. There was a waterfall on the edge of one side with big rocks to climb on. It was beautiful to see. Jackson and his friends were hiking through the woods when they stumbled upon the place. No one was around and it appeared quiet. Splashes from the falls were the only sounds heard.

"I've never seen this place before." Junior said as he admired his surroundings.
"Me either." Henry said.
"This is cool." John said.
"I know." Larry said.

The boys glanced around them taking in all the beauty. They had wondered who else knew about this place. It looked empty as if no visitors ever came.

"Let's swim in it." John suggested.
"Do you think we are allowed?" Larry asked.
"No one is around." Jackson replied.

As the boys began taking their shirts off, they were approached by an old woman who was walking through the woods. She was concerned about the boys being near the water.

"What are you boys doing?" The woman asked.
"We are going to swim." John replied.
"I wouldn't if I were you." The woman warned.

The boys stared at the woman in curiosity. They wasn't sure why the woman wouldn't want them in the water.

"Why not?" Jackson asked.
"Because of the little creatures." The woman replied with a strange look on her face.

Now they thought the woman was crazy. There couldn't be a little creature out in the water.

"Little creatures?" Junior asked.
"Yes, human like creatures that live out behind the falls." The woman replied.

The boys glanced over to the falls.

"I don't see anything." Jackson said.
"That's because they are hidden behind the falls." The woman said.
"Who are they?" John asked.
"Little men that were known to live out in the forest centuries ago." The woman began explaining.

This was hard for the boys to believe.

"They were eventually killed off over time, but it's said that a few survived." The woman explained.

The boys were silent as the woman continued. It was hard for them to comprehend the woman's story.

"They made a home behind the falls where they could stay hidden from others. They feed off the land and fish to survive. They don't want people here." The woman continued.

Jackson wasn't convinced.

"I don't believe you." Jackson said.

Ignoring Jackson's comment,

"When kids come to swim, the little creatures come after them. They don't want their only home invaded again like before. They come out at night when it's safe from other humans." The woman finished explaining as she walked off.

All five boys thought for awhile on what the old woman said. Jackson and Henry believed the story was made up. They had considered maybe the woman was just out to scare them.

"Let's swim out to the falls and look for our self." Jackson suggested.
"What if the little creatures get us?" John asked.
"You really believe little creatures exist?" Henry asked.
"They may." Larry replied.

After a few more moments,

"Fine, let's go see." Junior said.

The boys jumped into the water and swam out to the waterfall. They wanted to know if the story was true.

"Climb the rocks." Junior dared Jackson.

"You climb the rocks." Jackson responded.

"I'm not climbing the rocks. The little creatures might come out." Junior said.

"I'll climb the rocks and go see what is behind the waterfall." Henry volunteered.

Suddenly, little rocks came out of the waterfall. It took the boys by surprise.

"They are throwing rocks at us. I don't think they want us here." Larry said.

"I knew they were real. The woman was telling the truth after all." Junior said.

"The rocks are probably coming down the falls from the top." Jackson said.

"I'm checking this out now." Henry said.

Henry climbed up the big rocks and disappeared behind the falls. The others grew concerned.

"Where did you go?" Larry asked.

"Can you see anything?" Junior asked in curiosity.

"Henry." John whispered with concern.

Henry didn't answer them. He was too busy observing what was behind the falls. It was dark and quiet. There wasn't much he could see. That's until he began hearing something shuffling around. A closer look brought a frightening moment. Suddenly, Little shadow figures came towards him. Henry lunged through the falls out into the water. He landed next to his friends. He was panicking.

"They are coming!" Henry screamed.
"Swim now!" Jackson hollered.

Everyone swam back to the shore as fast as they could. As they walked out of the water, the boys looked behind them.

"I see something swimming towards us." Larry said.
"I think the little creatures are coming after us." Junior said.

They turned around to leave. No one wanted to stick around to see what came out of that water. They knew at this point that the woman's story had to be true.

"Get your stuff!" Larry yelled.
"Let's get out of here." Henry said.

The boys grabbed their shirts and took off running through the woods. No one stopped till they reached home. They never returned to the waterfall again.

CAMPING STORY

A weekend of Camping with family brought a scary night for Darrel and his cousins. The last night there, they decided to sit around the fire telling stories. After awhile, it came to Darrel's turn. His story would be the highlight of the evening.

"Two children were camping with their parents when they slipped away into the woods. Following paths, they picked apples from trees." Darrel began his story.

His cousins glanced around. They noticed three different paths near their camping site. They turned back to listen more.

"They came upon a lake. One of the children got too close to the water and fell in. The other child tried to save his sister, but they both ended up drowning." Darrel continued.

The cousins stared at Darrel with curiosity. They hadn't heard of such a story before.

"The parents buried them here at this lake and visited them until they died." Darrel ended.

Everyone wasn't sure what to think about Darrel's story. They wondered how true it really was.

"How true is this story?" Calvin asked.
"You see them three paths?" Darrel asked as he pointed at the same time his cousins turned to look.

The children all replied,

"Yes."

Darrel began speaking again.

"If you take the path to the left, you will see the lake they drowned in." Darrel said.

Renee and Brandy became scared. They held tightly onto each other while listening.

"If you take the path to the right, you will see the apple trees that withered away after the children died." Darrel continued.

Walter and Calvin were silently awaiting what the third path would bring. The story interested them.

"If you take the middle path, you will find the grave markings." Darrel finished.

The children looked at each other.

"Do you want to go check the paths out?" Darrel asked his cousins in hope of a good scare.
"No." Renee blurted out.

Darrel looked at her.

"Are you scared?" Darrel asked.
"It's dark." Brandy stepped in.

Everyone began having an input.

"We have flashlights." Walter said.
"We can pair up and each take a different path. It will be fun." Calvin suggested.

Renee was scared.

"What if we get lost?" Renee asked.
"We won't." Brandy replied.

After a few moments,

"Let's see how true this story is." Calvin said as he stood up to walk away from the group.

Everyone followed to the paths.

"Walter and Calvin, you take the path to the left and check out the lake. Renee and Brandy, you take the path to the right and check out the old apple trees. I will take the middle path and check out the grave markings." Darrel said.

The children paired up and began down their paths. No one knew why they had agreed to do this.

"It's scary out here." Renee said.
"We will just grab an apple and go back." Brandy said.
"Well let's hurry." Renee said.

The two searched around for the old apple trees. Finally, they found them.

"Look. Here's a half dried up apple." Brandy said.
"Great. Let's take it back." Renee said.

Renee and Brandy headed back to camp with their apple to show. They couldn't wait to get out of the woods. In the meantime,

"It's quiet out here." Walter said.
"Yes, I noticed." Calvin said.

The boys eventually made it to the lake. The wind was lightly breezy. The stars were very few.

"I guess this is where the drownings took place." Calvin said.

Suddenly, the boys began hearing sounds around them. They turned around quickly to look.

"Do you see anything?" Walter asked.

Staring into the darkness,

"No." Calvin replied.

After a few moments,

"We should head back." Walter suggested.

Walter and Calvin took the path back to camp. They walked fast watching their surroundings along the way. Going to Darrel, he was the brave one to take the middle path by himself.

"Here's the grave markings." Darrel said to himself.

Darrel bent down to observe the graves. After awhile, the wind began picking up.

"I should go back to camp now." Darrel whispered.

About that time, cries began through the woods. Darrel became scared and took off running. Realizing he shouldn't have gone off on his own, Darrel wanted to quickly get out of the woods. As he came out of the path, the others approached him.

"Why are you running?" Walter asked.
"I heard cries." Darrel replied.
"We heard noises by the lake." Calvin said.
"We didn't hear anything by the apple trees." Renee said.

They all stood talking to each other.

"It must have been the dead children." Darrel said.
"What do you mean?" Brandy asked.
"I forgot to tell you that the children's ghost haunts the woods." Darrel explained.

They swore to each other they would never take the paths again. They went to bed and left the area the next morning with their parents. It was a sleepless night for the cousins. They stayed awake in fear of the children's ghost coming to get them.

FROM BEYOND

The night frights,
Give a good scare,
Bring all your might,
If you dare.

When you go,
And you're not free,
Lay a little low,
To let it be.

Being brave,
Is not always tough,
But needing a save,
Can make it rough.

Be wide awake,
Challenges are on,
The ghosts await,
From far beyond.

www.ingramcontent.com/pod-product-compliance
Lightning Source LLC
LaVergne TN
LVHW020441070526
838199LV00063B/4811